COCKLES IS CONVENIENT

Cockles is Convenient

Bette Meyrick

Gomer Press
1981

First Impression—October 1981

ISBN 0 85088 615 5

©Bette Meyrick

Printed by J. D. Lewis and Sons Ltd.,
Gomer Press, Llandysul, Dyfed

To

NOEL

COCKLES IS CONVENIENT

Dear Reader,

If you are among those people who have momentarily found themselves stunned into a state of appalling doubt as to their sexual adequacy after having read of the gargantuan feats of sexual prowess so explicitly described in so many recent publications, where male and female alike accrue their successes like notches on a gun belt, then the following saga of events relating three traumatic months of my early life will, I hope, bring some solace.

Of course, I cannot, nay, dare not, offer any proof of the truth of the incidents related in this narrative, but, sufficient to say, I feel myself duty bound to caution any reader who, even while raising a sceptical eyebrow, might find himself, or herself, tempted to put the aphrodisiacal properties of the Welsh cockle to the test, that they might be starting an inexorable chain of events.

I therefore, hereby declare, that I wish to disclaim all responsibility for any cockle-less beaches in Wales and for any subsequent population explosion.

Signed:
Evan Evans, Draper Highclass
32 High Street
Llanporth

Quantum libet
Quantum sufficit

In hoc signo vinces!

Chapter 1

"Damn sun!" I muttered irritably as I felt under the polished mahogany counter for the stack of brown paper I kept there ready for just such an emergency. The telling pressure of the top button of my trousers as I bent down caused a fleeting moment of regret of accepting Myra's offer of a second helping of dumpling broth—not to mention the generous portion of apple and clove pie I'd topped it off with. That was the trouble with having such a good cook for a wife, I thought somewhat ruefully as I considered the threatened expansion of my waistline, and I made a mental resolution to ease off a bit otherwise I'd find myself ending up looking like Tanker Davis.

The transparent yellow sunblind which I had lowered that morning over the front window, cast a rich, golden glow as I climbed cautiously into the crammed window space, carefully placing one foot between the lace jabots and the cards of plain and fancy buttons, precariously balancing myself while I searched for another few square inches of space to rest my other foot. Three bolts of various striped flannelette which I had dexterously arranged on two spindly hat-stands the previous week, rocked ominously, threatening to crash down on my display of the latest Cardiff Fashion blouses as I desperately endeavoured to retain my tottering balance.

"Damn sun!" I muttered again, gingerly placing the toe of my boot on a pile of long, woollen underpants, as the only compromise available to avoid total collapsing disaster, the shortage of un-used space being somewhat acute in my artistically cluttered window.

I hadn't really intended to be a Draper. Always fancied myself as a Trawler Captain—in fact I'd quite enjoyed the years I'd spent on a destroyer during the Great War. But Pa had died suddenly, shortly after I'd returned home to court and marry Myra. Mam, to my surprise, had decided to go back to her old home and live with her sister in Clynderwen, and I just drifted into taking on the shop.

Mind you, I couldn't keep up with the tailoring—a really first-class tailor Pa had been, with the back parlour table always covered with half-made, tacked suitings and flimsy brown patterns, thousands of pins and pieces of slippery tailor's chalk and every chair piled high with remnants of best worsted and draped with half-sewn waistcoats and gaping armholed jackets awaiting the expert fitting of a well-tailored sleeve.

The intermittent chattering of the Singer treadle had punctuated my every childhood dream, for Pa worked long into the night after the shop was closed at half past five, while Mam expertly stiched the countless button-holes; and the bales of suiting sat heavily a-top my wardrobe, biding patiently until the confident slicing of Pa's outsize cutting scissors transformed them into masterpieces of tailoring.

Loved cloth he did—always smoothing his hand reverently over his lengths of material, serge and tweed, twill and herringbone, while the thought of wasting any was almost sacrilege, which doubtless accounted for the fact that I was continually bumping into customers sporting an Evans Suit made of the same material as my own short trousers!

No, there wasn't a hope in hell of my taking over the tailoring, so I had decided to compensate for the consequent drop in takings by helping out Dai Rees with a spot of Building and Decorating while Myra looked after the shop.

The women customers had nearly driven me mad, mind, when I'd first taken over the shop, but I soon began to see the lighter side of it, and with frequent sustaining visits to The Prince Albert and Snipper Jones the Barber for a bit of male company and chat, coupled with my excursions into the realms of Building and Decorating with my old school pal, Dai, life was quite interesting—especially when Mrs. Ruby Tyler called into the shop—lovely she was, with a slim, white throat that trilled up and down when she lifted her head to reach the high soprano notes at Choir practice.

Forcibly dragging my mind away from the undeniably attractive attributes of Mrs. Ruby Tyler, I started to pin the sheets of brown paper over the frocks and blouses, the bodices and latest cloche hats, the striped shirts and the bolts of cloth whose colours were threatened by the insidious fading properties of the strong sunlight, the golden sunblind giving but minimal protection against the full strength of the early afternoon's glaring rays. Mind you, we didn't have many really full-blooded, blistering hot days of undiluted sunshine down in that remote part of West Wales, the damp Atlantic air saw to that, and it was a damn good job too, otherwise I'd never be able to persuade the good ladies of Llanporth to part with their shillings by my tempting window displays—brown paper being not exactly the most alluring of window dressing materials!

A growing sense of being watched came over me as I pinned the last sheet over a particularly fetching, sleeveless, *crêpe-de Chine* blouse (look lovely on Mrs. Ruby Tyler it would). Carefully I twisted round, not daring to move my boots from their chosen positions, a smile all ready to greet a prospective customer waiting for me to open the shop after the Dinner-time Closing, but my smile faded slightly when I found the golden-hued, vacantly staring face of Dull Reggie pressed up against the window. I should have known, I thought with a grimace,—always stopped to peer closely into each window he did, as he ambled his slow-witted way happily back to the Board School to continue the already six pointless years he had spent there. Harmless he was, mind, but absolutely *twp*. What the hell he'd do when he finished his 'education' next year, I couldn't imagine—neither The Railway nor The Trawlers for certain, and what else was there? A bit of Council work he might manage, as long as they didn't give him the job of lighting the street lamps, blow himself up for sure he would—and us with him, and I made a mental note to warn Reynolds the Council about him.

"Hello Reggie," I mouthed slowly and with great facial exaggeration. Well, you couldn't help liking him—he was always so bloody happy! Six other young ones his Mam had to look after in the earth-floored cottage on the edge of the village, and another soon to arrive if the tension on her already outsize pinny was anything to go by when she last came into the shop for a bit of muslin. Casual work loading fish boxes his Pa did, and very casual at that too, as often he disappeared for weeks on end. Somebody said he had another wife and equally well proportioned family down Carmarthen way. God, I thought, he must be a bloody masochist, and only a frit of a fellow he was too, all skin and bone, and no wonder if he regularly managed to keep his two undeniably fertile wives so splendidly productive. I don't deny I fancy the ladies a bit myself, but that was damn ridiculous—almost suicidal, and anyway, Carmarthen was too far away!

Dull Reggie's broad face broke into a slow beaming smile of

pleasure at my mouthed greeting. His lazily focused eyes wandered bemusedly over my brown paper draped goods, then turning slowly, he ambled off down the dinner time deserted street, his hands hanging loosely at his sides, making for Lewis the Ironmongers, a few doors down, where he would stare in transfixed fascination at the buckets and kettles, shovels and hammers for a further few mind-glazed minutes before carrying on his way.

He was already nearly half an hour late for school I noticed as I took a quick look at Pa's pocket watch to see if it was time to open the shop for the afternoon session, but old Jenkins the Schoolmaster didn't trouble too much about him—as long as he showed up sometime before four o'clock, so as to be ready to go home, that was all that mattered.

Only another hour and a half before the train was due, I thought to myself with pleasurable anticipation as I flicked up the roller blinds on the two narrow shop doors and drew down the bolt. The village was gradually throwing off the deserted lethargy of the dinner hour, for only The Prince Albert and The Mariners had open doors between one and two o'clock, their friendly invitation contrasting with all the blankly shuttered shops in the road.

I turned to the counter to tidy away a few boxes of haberdashery, whistling quietly under my breath as I happily contemplated the spectacular effect the two purchases I was soon to collect from the station, would have on my lady customers. Fifty-five bob each they were going to cost me, but I had considered it a good investment when Cardiff Hughes had offered me the chance of two spare ones from his Emporium. Double your turnover inside two months he'd assured me as we'd stood in his dark, cramped little office behind the Millinery Department. And after having arranged that he would get the pair of them down to the railway sidings for the 11.35 Cardiff train so that Evans the Guard could slip them unobtrusively in to his van, the deal was settled,—after all, there was no point in paying G.W.R. delivery charges, was there? Not when you've got a pal right there in the Guard's van. I'd offered to let Mrs. Evans have her next pair of corsets at half price in return for the favour, but old Frank had said that he'd rather I stood him a couple of pints in The Prince

Albert, so that was what I intended to do after Choir Practice that night—thirsty work, singing, after all.

The grandfather clock in the back parlour was just striking three when I eventually hung my brown shop coat behind the passage door and donned my second best blue serge.

"Look after the shop, Myra," I called through the kitchen door, "just off down to the station to pick up a few orders," I explained as she appeared, rosy cheeked, from the garden. "There's lovely you look," I added involuntarily, commenting on the polka dot, afternoon frock she'd changed into. Her short, bobbed hair cheekily framed her small, lively face as she stood in the back kitchen doorway. I'd always liked her hair long, but she'd insisted that everybody would think she was old-fashioned if she hadn't had it cut into the latest short bob. I was getting used to it now, in fact I was quite beginning to like it, seemed to match the shorter skirts, somehow.

"Just let me finish damping down the clothes and I'll be there in a tick," she replied. "Damn old sun dried it all up too much," she went on, "dry as a bone it is—I needn't have bothered to mangle it all if I'd known it was going to be so hot."

Women! I thought. Either the washing was too wet or the damn stuff was too dry! There was no pleasing them.

I spent a few moments giving myself a final scrutinising look in the Customers' Hat Mirror as I settled my straw boater stylishly on my head, smoothing down my moustache as I admired my profile. Not bad, I thought to myself, not bad at all—for thirty. Myra was six years younger than me, and although we'd been married for going on five years there was no sign of any addition to our family. A few pointed comments we'd had mind—in fact, a grinning Dai even implied, when he'd wanted to get my goat, that certain parts of my anatomy, which I hold very dear, were filled with sawdust! Bloody nerve! But we weren't bothered—plenty of time, there was.

The warm September sun made my eyes squint as I stepped out onto the baked pavement, as hot as June it was, and lovely to get out of the musty atmosphere of the shop. Trade hadn't exactly been brisk that afternoon, and that dithering woman, Nellie Williams, had stood fidgeting for ages in front of the counter while I'd politely passed the time of day, enquired after her Billie, remarked on the unaccustomed good weather,

13

pointed out the latest fancy ribbons and lace and finally, in desperation, asked, and what can I do for you Mrs. Williams?

I knew she'd regretted coming in as soon as she'd opened the door and spotted me behind the counter instead of Myra. Three times she'd walked past, peering in to see who was serving, but the dark interior obviously afforded such an unco-operative contrast to the brilliant sunshine outside, that finally, deciding to take the bull by the horns, she'd pinged open the door only to stand in dismay when she'd realised that her gamble hadn't come off and that a male personage was waiting to serve her.

"Is Mrs. Evans about?" she'd managed to whisper after I'd run out of pleasantries. I'd known it was coming, of course. Knickers, vests, bodices, corsets—anybody would think I never knew that the damn things existed the way some of the women made such a fuss about buying them.

"I'm afraid not Mrs. Williams," I'd replied with great patience, "Just popped down to Rees the Farm for a jug of buttermilk—but I can be of assistance, I'm sure," I'd added with a re-assuring smile. "What was it you wanted now?" And I'd waited for the inevitable answer.

"Um . . . a . . . a small card of overall buttons please, Mr. Evans."—it was always a card of buttons or a reel of cotton or a small packet of needles as a substitute for whatever feminine requisites they really required. I think it was because I was a bit on the young side, compared to Pa. Our new, young doctor we shared with the neighbouring village was having the same trouble I'd gathered . . . "You can't tell him . . . *things*, Mabel," Miss Brown was heard to comment to her sister at the Church Whistdrive. "It's not right . . ."

Whatever Mrs. Williams did with the endless cards of overall buttons I couldn't imagine, her Billie's G.W.R. overalls must have the blessed things sewn all over them!

"Small packet of fasten patenters, Mr. Evans please," a blushing little Mrs. Phillips always asked for. I'd given up trying to tell her that they were called patent fasteners, because she always got it backwards the next time, just the same. In fact, I was almost beginning to think of them as fasten patenters myself—it had a curiously logical ring to it! "And when will Mrs. Evans be back, please?" as the small purchase

14

was deposited, lost and lonely, at the bottom of her enormous wicker basket.

Different from Mrs. Ruby Tyler now, a pleasure it was to serve her as she sat, crossed kneed on the Customers' Chair.

"Good morning, Evan," she'd crimson smile—even wore lipstick in the morning, mind. Myra never did that, only after dinner. Well, there was a time and place for everything, I suppose, but it looked lovely on Ruby any time.

"'Morning, Ruby," I'd answer, beaming all over my face. No calico, button-waisted drawers or sensible wollen underwear for her,—*crêpe-de-Chine* camiknickers, the very latest, she wore, although only her husband, Tyler the Customs, and myself knew it, of course. Oh yes, a real pleasure it was to serve Mrs. Ruby Tyler. Special boxes on the second shelf would be brought with a flourish to the counter and their carefully tissue-paper wrapped contents laid out in delicate pastel hues for her perusal.

I think I could safely say, without being too conceited, that she fancied me a bit. She never gave the correct money for her purchases—always had to have change pressed gently into her waiting open palms.

"Thank you Mr. Evans," she'd say slowly, or "Thank you, Evan," if she was feeling particularly friendly, looking deep into my eyes as she gracefully rose from the Customers' Chair, leaving the tantalising fragrance of California Poppy lingering on the shop air as she pinged her elegant way out. Real lovely she was, aye.

I'd subconsciously built up a League Table of my female customers over the seven years I'd been in the shop. All in the interests of business, of course—well, I had to make sure I was catering for all tastes as well as for all sizes. Bottom of The League, in fourth position were the magnificently boned, corsetted contingent with their wool or calico bloomers, (double gussetted, of course,) their heftily shouldered camisoles and black woollen stockings, their long stuff skirts—*Diawl!* They were almost Edwardian with their modesty vests to put inside the vee's of their blouses and flowered print wrap-around overalls—very wrap around they had to be too when those well corsetted hips grandly passed the 50 inch mark.

Third Place went to the salmon-pink, well-elasticated knickered variety, with cotton bodices and the occasional slightly less armourplated corset decorated with numerous appendages to keep up their cotton stockings which peeped daringly from under their heavy dark skirts—at least six inches above their ankles they were!

Second Place was filled with the short-legged rayon knickered, corseletted (non-boned) regiment with dark-toned cotton or rayon stockings, topped by quite modish waistless frocks over directoir petticoats. But pride of place at the Top of the League were the few delightful damsels who sported flesh-coloured stockings, lightly supported by incredibly narrow, elastic suspender belts; eau-de-nil artificial silk underwear—some with French Legs mind, and, of course, *crêpe-de-Chine* camiknickers. Their dresses hung beautifully straight and devastatingly short with a belt draped around their slim hips—for there were no outsize members of the First League—at least, I never had any amongst my customers. Only five there were in it anyway. Myra was in the Top League, of course, but she wouldn't wear French Legs—said they were too draughty.

I've gone into some detail regarding the various items appearing in each League, purely in the interests of the reader, as after seven years of catering mostly for female drapery, now that the Gent's Outfitting side had dwindled, I automatically found myself mentally placing any feminine acquaintance into one of the Four Leagues. Just a matter of habit, it was, after all.

"See you in Choir Practice tonight, Evan!" Davis the Coal waved from his cart as he jogged leisurely up the centre of the road as I closed the shop door behind me.

"I'll be there, boy!" I called back, envying him the coolness of his open-necked, collar-less shirt and rolled up sleeves. Stifling it was in my blue serge, but you had to look well turned out when you were a Clothier and Draper—Highclass, as the sign above the shop said. Bit of a trial it was at times, mind, keeping up appearances, which was one reason why I enjoyed helping Dai out with his Building and Decorating, really relaxing it was to don old clothes and overalls and do a bit of manual work for a change. Like leading a double life almost.

Two front doors on either side of the road , suddenly opened simultaneously as I started to make my way down the hill to the station, and out scurried Mrs. Terry and Mrs. Owen, (League

4 and 3 respectively), armed with bucket and shovel both making a bee-line for the still steaming pile of manure Davis the Coal's horse had just obligingly presented them with in the middle of the road. Now if I was on my Building and Decorating lark, I, too, could have availed myself of the opportunity of acquiring a bit of richness for the garden, but I couldn't dream of it when I was Dressed for Drapery. Appearances again, you see, so I had to content myself with raising my boater to the two intently shovelling ladies, wishing them a very good day and continue on my fertilizer-less way. Pity really. That damn horse, I reflected, never seemed to choose Building Days to deposit his magnificent odorous gift—same with Perry the Milk and Shorty Howes the Bread—their steeds always seemed to answer the call of Nature when I was refinely Dressed for Drapery. And, of course, Myra, being League 1, couldn't possibly nip out with a bucket and shovel, now could she? Fair play. Nothing to do with station in life, you understand—after all, some of my League 4 ladies were very well bred but thought nothing demeaning in their shovelling up a bit of goodness. Just mental attitude, really, I suppose, a bit old-fashioned they were.

"'Afternoon, there, Evan! Hot one today, mind." Lloyd the Stationmaster wiped his glistening forehead and gave a half suppressed onion-flavoured burp before adding, "See you in Choir tonight then?"

"I'll be there, boy," I replied once more with an acknowledging wave as I strode onto the afternoon quiet, bee-droning platform.

The little branch terminus shimmered in the heat. Golden marigolds and rich blue lobelia colourfully spelt out the name LLANPORTH in the neatly tended flowerbeds along both platforms, while chrysanthemums and gladioli, geraniums and flocks grew in profusion along the entire lengths, backed by the finest and longest vegetable strips in the whole of Pembrokeshire, which was the reason why Umshla Watkins the Porter rarely had any time for actual G.W.R. duties, as naturally he was always so busy tending the flower and vegetable gardens. Full time job it was, after all.

Any unfortunate traveller rash enough to arrive laden with luggage when it was Umshla's hoeing time, or planting time, or digging time or watering time, was doomed to fend for himself. The best runner beans I've ever tasted grew along the platform edge, behind the peony bushes, and Umshla's rhubarb had to be seen to be believed—like a forest of pink treetrunks it was. And it was not a bit of good anyone looking for a handcart to help move a heavy trunk. Full of potatoes, turnips, carrots, peas, lettuce, rhubarb and various other Platform Produce, they both were, ready for Umshla to wheel round the village to sell to eager housewives. For inspite of each small, highly cultivated back garden behind the terraced houses of the village, Railway Rhubarb and all other produce was always in great demand. The quality was undeniable, the price very reasonable, and the flavour delicious—something to do with the richness of the soil being so close to the Railway, everybody said. All that sulphur and smoke must do something! And as Davis the Coal's horse and cart were often parked for hours down by the coal sidings, that also, no doubt had something to do with the richness of the soil, as there's always a bucket and shovel handy on a railway.

Old Lloyd the Stationmaster took it all as a matter of course that Umshla would rarely, if ever, be available for any actual Company work. After all, he had to get his priorities right,— and providing Mrs. Lloyd with free vegetables and flowers, and splitting the profits of the sales with Umshla, half each, no messing, were two decisive factors in keeping the G.W.R. Market Garden flourishing.

"S . . . s . . . s . . . see . . . see . . . s . . . s . . ."

"Yes, boy," I hurriedly interrupted before Umshla could get himself further tangled up with his stuttering, "See you tonight at Choir." and he grinned back as he loosened a few weeds with his hoe, quite accustomed to everyone reading his mind after every stuttering start to any remark he set about uttering.

But a lovely tenor he was—not a sign of a stutter or a stammer once he opened his mouth to sing. As an experiment he'd once tried singing his way through life, but somehow, it didn't seem to work with ordinary, everyday words. And as Allelujahs, "Praise be to Zion", and "Baal, we cry to thee", don't come into ordinary conversation very often, the experiment was a failure! So he had to content himself with relying on everyone reading his mind once he'd managed to get out the initial few words to put them on the right track. But tamping mad he got, mind, if you misunderstood what he meant—even threw a bunch of carrots in exasperation at poor Mrs. Blackmore because she kept offering him a cup of tea or a drink of water from her can, when he was on one of his selling rounds—when all he was desperately trying to ask was to avail himself of her lav at the top of the garden!

The Stationmaster sent him back to apologise, of course, after an irate Mrs. Blackmore had marched onto the platform and stormed into his office to voice her complaint at being the target for a bunch of earth-clogged carrots. But poor old Umshla had taken so long trying to stammer out an apology on her front step, that she'd shut the door on him in despair! But he got on well with plants—and Cy Lloyd the Choirmaster.

The small, local tank engine came steaming noisily round the bend by Rees's Farm, full of its own importance as it pulled into the Arrival Platform with its two Third Class carriages, its single First Class carriage and its Guard's van. An automatic check with my watch confirmed that old Horace Llewellyn the Driver had brought her in dead on time, and I gave him an appreciative wave as he slowly steamed past to the buffers.

Three passengers climbed out of the Third Class compartments into the bright sunshine and Captain Rees-Williams, Merchant Navy Retired, descended grandly from the First Class, sweltering in his expensive Harris Tweed as he turned to help an elegant young lady from his compartment. Now who the hell was this beautiful creature, I thought to myself with some puzzlement as I walked towards them, making my way to the Guard's Van. Well, damn me, I thought, as realisation suddenly dawned, if it wasn't young Selina, the old man's daughter. Talk about a transformation —the last time I'd seen her she'd been encased in the copious, long pleats of a green serge school uniform gymslip and sensible hat of the near-by Grammar, and here she was now, but a few weeks later, in an oyster linen, slip of a dress and a crocodile handbag! Very fetching indeed, very fetching, and I recalled that Mrs. Rees-Williams had meticulously gone to a great deal of trouble to inform all the village that Selina was spending the summer 'abroad'. 'It does them good to broaden their horizons before going up to University, I always say,' and we'd all agreed that we always said it too, and off to France Selina had gone with an obscure maiden aunt from Wrexham. After all, she had passed her C.W.B. and her Higher with flying colours, we'd all read the announcement in the paper—twice. 'Going to get a Cap and Gown in Aberystwyth, she is, I hear,' little Mrs. Lily Phillips had confided in the shop in a hushed, reverend tone, yet obviously not quite sure why everyone was so impressed by Selina Rees-Williams buying clothes in Aberystwyth when there was a perfectly good Drapers Shop in Llanporth! Well, Mrs. Phillips or Lily Jones, as she then was, hadn't got past Standard Five in the Board School, and never learnt fractions, so you couldn't expect her to know the finer points of the ornamental vestments of higher education, after all. 'My sister once bought a pair of shoes in Cardiff,' she'd added as an afterthought as she was going out through the shop door. Well, there was just no answer to that now was there?

"Porter! Our cases!" rapped out Captain Rees-Williams, Retired, glaring imperiously at Umshla Watkins who was now busily engrossed in watering his marigolds. Umshla looked up from his task in surprise, the water sprinkling over his boots as he stood staring at the Captain in open-mouthed disbelief that he should actually be expected to for-go looking after the welfare of his precious plants in order to carry anything.

"I. . .I. . .I. . .I. . .mu. . .mu. . .must. . .I. . .must. . ." and he pointed in explanation to his flowerbeds.

"Our suitcases, man!" impatiently interrupted the increasingly irate, Harris tweeded figure, rapping the side of the open carriage door with his silver knobbed walking stick.

"B . . . B . . . But . . . but . . . I . . . I . . . but I . . ." and with that over rushed Lloyd the Stationmaster, brushing past me in haste, having realised the arrival of an important personage by the rare fact that a door of a First Class Compartment was open.

"Allow me, Captain Rees-Williams," he interpolated with a placating smile. After all, he didn't want any complaints to the Company, and within seconds the somewhat mollified Captain and his enchanting daughter were following a heavily laden Stationmaster to the exit where Mrs. Rees-Williams was waiting in their 16 h.p. De Dion Bouton, while Umshla gave them a friendly smile, touched his cap respectfully and carried on with his watering.

"Good-afternoon, Captain Rees-Williams," I volunteered as the trio strode past, but was only rewarded with an inarticulate grunt. Miserable bugger, I thought—"Good-afternoon Miss Rees-Williams" I tried again, raising my boater and flashing her one of my best smiles, glad, for once, I was Dressed for Drapery.

"Er. . .good-afternoon, Mr. . .ehm. . .Mr. . .ehm. . ."

Well, blow me! I thought, feeling my ego visibly deflate, she couldn't even remember my name! Ah well, you can't win 'em all, I decided philosophically, as I turned to watch the sylph-like figure disappear through the gate. Definitely League One —what a transformation!

"Evan! Evan!" The imperative cry interrupted my sad reflections and I turned to see Evans the Guard wildly gesticulating at me from his Van door.

"You didn't tell me they were going to be naked!" he gasped, rushing up to meet me. "Good God, man, you'll have me locked up!" I stood still in my tracks and stared uncomprehendingly at his hot, flustered face.

"What the hell are you talking about?" I asked, momentarily baffled.

"Your damn models—naked they are—all of them. I tell you, I've never been so embarrassed!" and he wiped his red face with his handkerchief while looking furtively up and down the platform.

"Didn't Cardiff Hughes wrap them up then?" I queried with a laugh as understanding dawned.

"Why no—not a stitch have they got on. I'll tell you," he repeated, "I've never been so embarrassed. I've got a spare mailbag on one of them, come and see, but the other two I've tried to hide behind the empty rabbit boxes, in case any of the younger, unmarried men—you know—well—you know . . ." he finished off lamely with an expressive shrug of the shoulders.

I gave a grin. If the younger, unmarried chaps were anything like they were when I was in that category, they wouldn't exactly be shocked or intrigued by the sight of unclothed shop models, but Old Frank was a bit straight-laced, fair play—and out of touch to say the least, seeing as it must be over forty years since he, himself, was a strictly Victorian-minded, young and unmarried youth. In a world of his own, he was, shut up by himself in that little van day after day, chewing his cloves.

"And Mrs. Evans wouldn't like it at all if she knew I'd travelled all the way from Cardiff with three naked women in my van," he added, a worried frown crossing his flushed face as he hurried back down the platform.

"They're only models, man," I pointed out, suppressing a smile with great difficulty. "And there's only supposed to be two, anyway."

"You try and explain that to Mrs. Evans—just you try!" he called over his shoulder as he climbed back into the van. I had a brief, mental picture of outsize Mrs. Evans (League 4) in full cry and reluctantly conceded he might have a point there!

The air was heavy with the smell of dead rabbit, day old chicks, dusty mailbags and Frank Evans' sardine sandwiches as I stood in the doorway waiting for my eyes to accustom themselves to the gloom.

I'd been looking forward to this moment for two weeks as I hadn't actually viewed my purchases before—only had them described, very eloquently, by Cardiff Hughes, and I hoped they were going to be as good as he'd promised. I knew they were second hand, but I didn't want anything tatty with bits chipped off, after all. With commendable restraint I had managed to keep my investment a secret from everyone, except Frank. Not even Myra knew what great things I was planning for the ladies of Llanporth. Surprise would bring the greatest impact, I felt sure, and when my elegantly attired models appeared overnight in the shop window, I knew it would be the talked of event of the week. *Diawl!* I might never be able to get rid of Dull Reggie peering in the window then! Waiting for them to move, he'd be!

Two pale, aristocratic faces, looking disdainfully over the tops of the empty rabbit boxes, gradually swam into my vision and I stared back, in fascination, at the beautiful, blank eyes, primly puckered, pink lips and gleaming bare shoulders as Frank continued to mutter about the sooner they're out of his Van the better he'd be pleased. Eagerly I started to clear a path to my long-awaited pair of prize beauties, carelessly scattering a *mêlée* of rabbit boxes behind me.

"Steady on, man, we'll have no place to move if you throw them about like that," cautioned Frank, "Help me lift them out and stack them on the platform first."

Controlling my impatience with difficulty I started to hand

the empty boxes back to Frank who heaved them out onto the platform and methodically stacked them up gainst the sunbaked wall, pausing only to allow a smiling Umshla to pass for a refill of his watering can from the stand tap by the Stationmaster's Office.

As the last box was heaved perspiringly out of the van we both stood back, breathing hard—more from the dusty, dry heat than from actual exertion.

"See what I mean now, do you?" muttered old Frank, shakily taking off his Guard's Cap and wiping the sweaty band dry while his blinking gaze rested on the now fully revealed feminine forms at the back of his van. Cool and elegant they looked, with gently swelling curves and slim aristocratic legs, and not a chip off anywhere, I gleefully noticed.

"If the Inspector had seen them I'd be in for it now, and no mistake—sure to be a G.W.R. rule against carrying unwrapped goods like this about—and them not paid for neither!" And he blanched at the thought and took a swift, wary glance up and down the deserted platform.

"Where's this extra one, then?" I asked and my eyes followed Frank's shakily pointing finger to a darkly outlined, mailbagged creature, propped drunkenly in the far corner, balancing on the heel of one of her unbelievably slender legs which protruded from beneath His Majesty's Mail.

"Well, you can take her back to Cardiff, I didn't order her." I declared. Frank stared at me in horror at the thought.

"Not me, boy!" he announced flatly, "they're all leaving my van right now and they'll not put another foot inside again —not unless they're wrapped and paid for." Adamant he was. I thought for a moment, well, as there was no question of my paying for a return journey for the unfortunate lady, it looked as if I was stuck with her. I made a quick calculation and decided that I'd write and offer Cardiff Hughes seven pounds for the three, while a plan for recovering some of the money was already beginning to shape in my mind. I'd put drunken Tabitha there in the corner out to work!

"Well, come on!" Frank's over anxious voice interrupted my thoughts. "They can't stay by 'ere no more—shunted into the sidings we'll be in half an hour." he added with a confirmative look at his pocket watch.

"But I thought they'd be wrapped up, man," I replied, "I

was going to carry them up to the shop one at a time, like a parcel. But I can't do that now. I'll tell you what,'' I suggested after a moment, ''I'll put 'em in the Waiting Room until I go and fetch an old sheet.''

''You can't do that, man! Why no, you can't do that.'' Frank panicked, ''Don't forget there are a few unmarried men about like,'' and he paused to give an embarrassed cough. ''It wouldn't do, would it?''

''Umshala . . . Umshala . . . um, shall I . . . um, shall I cut . . . um, shall I cut some . . .'' The pair of us swung round guiltily at the sudden, unmistakable voice at the open van door where Umshla Watkins, secateurs in hand, was stammering his way through an offer to cut some flowers for Mrs. Evans, when his flow slowed to a gradual halt as he blinked unbelievingly at the sight of the dim, creamy white, female forms standing at the back of the van. A deep, ruddy flush crept up over his neck and face and he gulped noisily.

'Young' Umshla was thirty five if he was a day, I mean, he'd been ready to go up to the Big Class with Old Jenkins when I'd only started in The Babies Room. He'd acquired his nickname within months of starting school as it had always repeatedly prefaced any remark he'd made to old Miss Harris. It was 'um shall I do this' and 'um, shall I do that'. 'Um shall I clean the blackboard?' and 'Um shall I tidy the books?' The constant, merciless teasing he'd received from the girls had driven him to regard them with dismay and dread. Never had anything to do with them ever since—never went behind the Cricket Shed or down the back lane to experiment with the rest of us and never went to the Church Socials or Dances when he grew up. He'd go to the Whistdrive, Supper and Dances, mind, but only for the Whistdrive and Supper, disappear he would then, tiptoeing out in his polished G.W.R. boots, leaving the rest of us to trip the patent-leather fantastic round the hall, without his ever having raised his eyes to his whist partner, leave alone actually look at any of the bobby dazzlers arrayed in their party finery.

Devoted almost all his loving attentions to his beautiful flowers and vegetables, the remainder he divided between his choir-singing and his widowed Mam, who was, even now, no doubt, up to her elbows in flour and raisins, in their hot little kitchen, preparing his favourite tea of hot welshcakes. Really doted on him she did—and why not, fair play? A lovely chap he

24

was really. Damned if I can remember his proper christian name now. Only his Mam ever used it. What was it now? . . . Cecil. That was it—Cecil Watkins. Doesn't sound right at all somehow.

He looked first at Evans the Guard, who was flustered as hell and trying ineffectively to position himself to block Umshla's line of vision and then over at me and back again to our nude feminine companions. And before we could say a word of explanation Umshla backed dazedly out of the van, his right hand spasmodically clicking his secateurs.

"Now look what you've done!" hissed a now desperate Frank. "If he tells his Mam and she tells Mrs. Evans . . . *Uffern Dân!* I should never have agreed to pick them up unofficial. Fool to myself I am." And he clasped his head in despair. Really lead on he did then. "If you'd had the damn things delivered properly in the first place, this would never have happened—Parcel Office would never have accepted them if they hadn't been decently wrapped up—but me—fool—me—just accepted them from this pal of yours down in the goods sidings. Fool to myself I am . . ." and he glared accusingly at the gently rounded figures standing silently through his tirade. Suddenly he grinned . . . "They're nice, though, aren't they, boy?" and he gave a hefty nudge in the direction of my ribs. "Nice and smooth like . . ." and he ran his hand down a cool, silky flank. "Bit different shape from Mrs. Evans, mind," he added with a poignant sigh. Although, from what I'd heard, he hadn't actually *seen* Mrs. Evans for over twenty years, not even by candlelight, but from the vast size of her frocks it didn't take much guesswork to know how much was underneath. She'd always been a big woman, I'd remembered Pa saying, it was what had attracted Frank to her in the first place, at the char-a-banc Chapel Outing to Bethesda Pool over thirty years before. Like a shapely, rosy-cheeked Amazon she'd been, with her frilled, high-necked blouse and long stiff skirt—and a twinkle in her eye to go with it. Oh, you and your twinkles, Mam had interrupted with a tut, when Pa had reminisced—but the twinkle had gone, long ago. Times change, and the four children hadn't helped much neither. Sid and Dave had both been killed within a month of each other on the Somme, and Mary and Martha had moved away and were busy raising their own families down in the Valleys somewhere. They never

25

saw them. Aye, it must be hard to keep a twinkle going, fair play, I thought, as Frank gave a rueful slap on the slim behind of the disdainful brunette and looked over at me.

"Well, come on then," he repeated, "What are you going to do with 'em?"

"What time is this train due out again, Frank?" I asked, a plan beginning to form at last.

"Six fifteen tomorrow morning. Why?"

"Great." I replied." Our best bet is to leave them where they are until it gets dark—you just close the van door and they can go over to the sidings and I'll pick them up after Choir Practice tonight."

"I'll have to have my mailbag off her, though," he pointed out with a nod in the direction of tipsy Tabitha.

"You do that then, boy, and I'll go and have a quiet word in Umshla's ear—tell him it's all a secret and he's not to breathe a word to anybody—especially his Mam!" And old Frank gave me a grateful look—well, very friendly with Mrs. Evans, Umshla's Mam was.

What the hell's the treatment for shock, I thought with an inward grin, as I walked across to the chrysanthemum bed to find 'young' Umshla Watkins, whose secateurs still seemed to be working overtime—well, letting off steam I suppose he was.

Chapter 2

I turned into Dai's builder's yard with a thankful sigh. Thank God it was only half way up the hill, I thought, regaining my breath after having pushed little Bertha Gwillam's magnificent baby carriage up the first steep slope for her. What the deuce these women wanted to go and buy such enormous heavy prams for I couldn't imagine—damn it—she couldn't even see over the top of it when the hood was up, and she always had to wait for somebody to give her a hand up the bottom half of the hill.

"Serve her right," Myra had commented somewhat scathingly, "why couldn't she go and get an ordinary pram or borrow Mrs. L. Y. T. Jones's like every body else? But no—not her—had to go and buy the biggest and best from Swansea, just to show off, and now," she ended with a chuckle, "she can't push the damn old thing up the hill—and the baby not ten pounds yet neither!"

I had managed, without too much difficulty, to explain to Umshla the circumstances surrounding the contents of the Guard's Van, and had impressed upon him the need for a bit of discretion—for Frank's sake—regarding my models. I hadn't actually waited long enough to hear what he had to say, but I gathered, from the first few stuttered utterances and the repeated shaking of his head, that as far as Umshla was concerned, he'd seen nothing in Frank's van except mailbags and rabbit boxes. I'd thought I might as well pay a call on old Dai, just to pass the time of day, seeing as I couldn't take my purchases back to the shop. The rhythmic sound of planing betrayed his presence in the Coffin Shed as I stood sweltering in the dusty, heavily lime-laden air of the builder's yard. Damn it was hot—more like June than September—nobody had even started thinking about winter-wear, leave alone buying it yet, I though morosely. Not a bit of good for trade these Indian Summers.

"How's it going then, Dai? How's your love life?" I called through the open doors. The aromatic smell of freshly planed elm drifted into my nostrils as I rustled my way through the ankle deep shavings littering the floor, the pale, curling slivers tangling themselves curiously about my boots.

Dai looked up from his task in surprise, pausing

automatically to remove a few shavings from the escapement of his long smoothing plane.

"Hullo there, Evan,—what you doing here then? Thought you were Drapering today. Bloody hot, isn't it?" he commented, wiping his glistening forehead with the back of his hand.

No wonder all the girls just fell at his feet, I thought grudgingly as I viewed the tall, tanned frame and mop of thick, curly hair. Good looking bugger he was, I had to admit and he had this compelling way with women—adored him they did. I didn't do too badly myself, of course, but when Dai was about I always found myself beaten to second place—bane of my life he'd been. I'd kept Myra well away from him in our courting days I don't mind telling you!

"I'll tell you a bit of good news now then, Evan," he announced grandly, pausing to reach for the thick earthenware jug of buttermilk he kept in his emergency coffin, along with his bottles of French polish and linseed oil. He took a long, appreciative swallow and proceeded to divulge his interesting bit of news as I gratefully took the proferred jug and refreshed my own dry throat with the exquisite sharp tartness.

"I've managed to talk old Rees the Farm into selling me that bit of land behind the yard at last!" he announced triumphantly. "Caught him in a weak moment down at The Mariners last night, when he was well tanked up."

"Well done, man, well done, boy!" I repeated in genuine admiration of his achievement, for I knew that Dai, and his Pa before him, had been after extending the yard for donkey's years, but wily old Rees the Farm couldn't be persuaded to part with a single blade of grass from the luxuriant pasture behind the High Street.

"What's it going to cost you then?" I asked, full of eager inquisitiveness.

"Twenty-five quid and a free coffin of best elm for Old Mam Rees when her time comes." replied Dai, punctuating his words with grunts as he re-commenced his forceful planing of the ominous 6ft. 6ins. of elm before him.

"Couldn't get more than eighty feet out of him though," he complained, "I could have done with a hundred at least. But we'll see, we'll see . . ." he finished with a knowing wink as he paused in his exertions to examine the blade of the plane suspiciously.

"Aw, eighty feet's not bad, fair play, Dai," I pointed out as he started to remove the offending plane iron for sharpening.

"Coming to stake it out this very afternoon, he is. Then I'll be able to move all those damn chickens up to the top end and keep a pig or two. Knock up a couple of sheds and I'll be able to carry a bigger stock of materials instead of having to trapse off to Haverfordwest every five minutes. Wearing the damn tyres out on the lorry I am."

A shadow, suddenly blocking the dusty sunlight streaming through the open doors, made us both turn to find old Rees the Farm about to greet us, his breeches tucked into his earth-caked gaiters, his flanelette, collarless shirt hanging open to the waist. Rough and ready old Rees was. Never wore a collar—not even to Chapel or The Mariners. "I've never sold that man a collar in all the years I've been drapering," Pa used to say. "In fact, he actually sold *me* sixteen old collarstuds belonging to his Pa—and I didn't want the damn things! Clever he is, mind!"

"Ready, are we?" he questioned, holding up a heavy, leather bound tape in Dai's direction.

"Hang on a minute," acknowledged Dai, laying the plane iron down beside a gleaming black oilstone. "I'll just find a couple of stakes," and he rootled through a pile of off-cuts in the corner of the Coffin Shed, found a couple of suitable pieces, expertly adzed them to a point, picked up a mallet and followed old Rees out into the yard.

"No need to go round to the gate," he called as Rees started to make his way back out onto the road. "We'll get through the fence at the back." He strode towards the high, rickety old fence and gave a few hefty kicks at the creosoted wood. "Won't be needing this by 'ere any more anyway," he remarked with a grin, and within seconds a splintered gap appeared revealing the lush, green pasture beyond. The Promised Land it must have looked to old Dai, I thought as the three of us scrambled through the jagged opening, treading down the tall stinging nettles growing high along the line of the fence. The air in my nostrils suddenly seemed fresh and moist as the deep, sweet scent of the thick, luxuriant grass and rich earth beneath contrasted with the dusty dry-baked yard behind us. Like different worlds they were, with only a rickety old fence to divide them.

"Eighty feet it is, then—and brass handles on the coffin, mind," Old Rees established, ineffectively flicking at a couple of flies hovering before his face.

"Right you are," agreed Dai, "the very best you shall have."

I gazed across the vast expanse of field—a good ten acres it must have been. Why Old Rees was so reluctant to part with more than eighty feet I couldn't see—a drop in the ocean it would be after all.

"You hold the end of the tape and I'll measure it out and hammer the stakes in," suggested Dai, wide eyed with innocence.

"No bloody fear!" counteracted Rees, "You hold the bloody tape and I'll do the measuring and staking!" and he took the mallet and stakes from Dai's hand and offered him the end of the tape. I managed to suppress a chuckle at Dai's abortive attempt to wangle a few extra feet—but surely he hadn't expected Old Rees to fall for that one!

"All the same to me, boy," announced Dai with an amicable shrug of the shoulders, "but there's suspicious you are!" he admonished with a grin. But Rees just grunted sceptically as he watched Dai squat down by the corner of the fence and place the brass-looped end of the tape up against the boundary.

"Got it right now, have you?" Rees peered down amongst the nettles to check the position and satisfied that Dai wasn't trying to gain a few extra inches, he started to stride out across the field, unwinding the tape as he went.

"A great day it is for you, boy," I commented, "You've got it at last." I switched my gaze from Rees's retreating back down to the crouched figure at my feet, but Dai was too intent on manipulating a long piece of twine from his pocket to bother with a reply. I watched, intrigued, as deftly he threaded one end of the twine through the brass loop on the end of the tape and quietly let the remainder play out. I watched hypnotised, as the tape slowly crept away from us as old Rees continued to stride on.

"You crafty bugger!" I murmured with admiration as Dai winked up at me.

"He won't miss an extra fifteen feet or so," he pointed out reasonably, "And I'll carve a couple of Tudor roses on the coffin as a bonus for Old Mam Rees," he added, as he raised his hand in acknowledgement as Rees turned to check that he was still backed tight to the fence. Real suspicious he was—as Dai had said!

The loop of twine continued to trail out slowly, the end of the tape now completely gone from sight amongst the thick grass, when old Rees came to a halt, turned and raised his hand.

"That's it!" he shouted back and proceeded to hammer in the stake, lazily watched, with idle curiosity, by a herd of cud-chewing Jerseys. Within seconds the deed was done, for better or for worse, and he came walking back to us, winding the tape as he went. When he'd covered about a third of the distance Dai nonchalantly released one end of the twine to allow it to slip out of the brass loop, quietly gathered it up and replaced it in his back pocket.

"Haven't sold me short now, have you?" he joked accusingly as Rees drew up.

"Want to check it your bloody self then?" Rees retorted, looking highly outraged.

"Why no, boy," appealed Dai, refusing the proferred tape, "Only joking, I was . . . if you say it's eighty feet then eighty feet it is—I'll stake my life on it!" And he clapped Old Rees on the back with matey cameraderie while I turned away desperately trying to hide the broad grin which I completely failed to keep off my face at such cheerful blatancy!

The same procedure was carefully repeated from the opposite corner of the back fence, with Dai whistling happily away under his breath. Didn't know the meaning of nerves! Old Rees could be a nasty bugger if anyone crossed him, mind—he'd even horse-whipped old Dago Jones in no mean fashion, only last winter, for poaching on his land.

"How do you know you've allowed the same length on both sides?" I whispered cautiously as Dai replaced the twine in his pocket for the second time.

"I cut it off at thirty-two feet, see. Gives me about fifteen feet when it's let out—allowing for a bit to hold onto like . . . prepared I was mind!" he added with a grin. "Cash on the nail, it is then," he greeted Old Rees as we clambered back through the broken fence.

The two of them faced each other in the hot, dusty yard. Rees brought a crumpled Bill of Sale out of his breeches' pocket and Dai pulled out five crisp, white fivers, two screws and the tangle of twine out of his back pocket.

"Look at this lot," he tutted with apparent exasperation, "if I'm not cluttering up my pockets with nails and screws, its bits of string!"

"Aye, I'm just as bad, boy," agreed Rees, as I grew hotter under the collar every second at the sight of the incriminating twine.

"What the hell I put that in there for I can't think," Dai went on as he discarded it carelessly on a heap of rubble behind him while I feverishly fumbled for a fag to steady my frayed nerves. Don't push your luck any further, I prayed, for God's sake leave it! Always the bloody same he was—couldn't resist the thrill of pushing something to the limit. Get himself hanged he would, one day—and me with him, I didn't doubt.

The fivers and Bill of Sale exchanged hands, the two shook hands soberly, clapped each other on the back, agreed that it had been a pleasure to do business and, at last, the transaction was completed.

There's a heartfelt sigh of relief I let out as Old Rees finally disappeared out through the gate, I can tell you. I turned to congratulate Dai, but he was already back at the hole in the fence, viewing his newly acquired property with a beatific beam of satisfaction on his face.

"What if he ever comes back to check the measurements?" I pointed out as I stood beside him.

"Don't you worry, boy—he'll never bother to do that." And he was right.

Mind you, there was a bit of perplexed head scratching went on down in the Council Offices nearly thirty years later, when they decided to build a housing estate on Old Rees's field. The surveyors were back and fore with their tapes and plans umpteen times. But Old Rees was long dead by then, so they reluctantly resigned themselves to amending their drawings and four council houses inexplicably found themselves with back gardens 15ft shorter than the remainder of the estate!

But Old Mam Rees did have her Tudor Roses—four beauties they were. Fair play!

"I'm glad you dropped in this afternoon, Evan." We were

both sitting on a coffin having a welcome smoke after the business of the day.

I looked over at Dai through a lovely haze of blue smoke. "Old Jenkins the Schoolmaster sent Dull Reggie down, earlier on, with a note asking if I could go and fix new hinges on the top of the sliding glass partition up at the school. Dangerous, he said it was. Be a pal and nip up to see to it for me, will you? I want to get that land roughly fenced in by tonight. I've got the wire and posts all ready this morning."

"Don't be daft, man," I answered, somewhat put out. "I can't go up there fixing hinges like this—Dressed for Drapery, I am, aren't I?" and I brushed a few remaining specks of rabbit-box dust off the knees of my second best blue serge trousers.

"Here," he directed, leaning backwards to catch hold of a grimy suit of very off-white overalls, hanging on a coffin handle, "You can put these on."

I considered the suggestion for a moment.

"Only take you half an hour, it will," he coaxed. Well, it was certainly more tempting than going back to the shop—and Myra wouldn't be expecting me back anyway.

"Aw, all right then," I agreed. "By the way—I want to borrow your hand-truck tonight," I added as I thankfully rid myself of the encumbrance of my blue serge jacket and waistcoat and gratefully pulled off my tie and stiff collar. There's lovely it felt as I twisted my neck round with relief at the unshackled freedom of a collarless shirt.

"Tonight?" Dai repeated in surprise. "What's on tonight then? Aren't you going to Choir Practice?" he asked in some wonder, as he stopped rootling around in the depths of his oak chest for suitable screws and hinges for the school partition.

"'Course I'm going—but I've got these special goods to pick up from the railway sidings afterwards—I'll tell you about it when I come back," I promised as I hung my trousers up by their braces and climbed into Dai's Painters' and Decorators' Overalls—lovely and loose and cool they were—a real treat. Pocketing the necessary screws and hinges, I picked up the tool frail and cast my eyes about outside for a suitable ladder.

"Where's the bloody ladder this time, then?" I shouted back through the door. Always leaving it somewhere, he was—'Don't mind if I leave my ladder in your back garden till

33

tomorrow, do you, Mrs. Harris? Save carrying it back to the yard.' he'd entreat, full of charm. 'Why no, 'course not Dai—any time,' would come the inevitable reply from Mrs. Harris, Mrs. Owen, Mrs. L. Y. T. Jones, Mrs. Griffiths and all his other admirers. I told you—he had this way with women—no matter how old—or young, they were. I forgot to mention that all these good ladies had very attractive daughters sleeping in very accommodating back bedrooms, by the way. How he managed to keep awake all day—leave alone work— with such strenuous activities and lack of sleep at night, I never could fathom. I just had to admit—he was a better man than me, no two ways about it. The sooner he got married the better —for everybody's peace of mind! Not that I'd ever heard anybody complain, mind. Very circumspect, Dai was. Managed to keep everybody either ignorant of his goings on or deliriously happy, as the case may be. Well, if he could fool Old Rees, he could fool anybody, fair play! Sometimes I even wondered if his own left hand knew what his right hand was doing!

"The ladder?—oh its up at Tŷ Mawr. Wants the whole place painted top to bottom and his boundary wall repaired, Old Rees-Williams," he announced with some satisfaction. I had a sudden mental picture of young Selina, beautiful young Selina, as she'd stepped off the train that very afternoon. Aw Gawd! I thought, he always seems to have everything laid on—the lucky bugger. I bet she sleeps in the back. "Take the small one from behind the chicken run." The reply interrupted my chain of thought. I took a deep sigh and resignedly rambled over to the heat-dazed chickens and yanked the ladder from behind their pen. There was an indignant flurry of feathers and chorus of clucks as the netting wire caught on the rungs. "Aw—shut up!" I growled—but only jealous, I was—just temporarily—it was the freedom of choice, see? That's all. Nothing to do with Myra, at all—wouldn't change her for the world—why no. More in the line of supplementary benefits I was thinking of really. Just give me half a chance boy—just half a chance.

I left Dai, armed with hammer, nails, roll of wire and the first two momentous posts, disappearing through the gap in the fence.

"See you later boy!" he shouted over his shoulder, "A real

pal you are!'' He never spoke a truer word, I thought, as I balanced the ladder and tool frail on my shoulder and manipulated my way out through the gate. A real Jekyll and Hyde, me, I thought as I whistled my overall-clad way up the High street, pausing briefly to give a passing slap on the generously plump backside of Rosie George, (League 3 with leanings to League 2) as she bent to pick up her water can from the pump—now you can't do thing like that when you're Dressed for Drapery, now can you? Makes a lovely change from politely raising your hat!

"Thee you at Choir tonight then, Mr. Evanth," she lisped after having let out a surprised shriek of delight at my friendly greeting. Pronounced it 'Koyah' she did—real Welshy—only moved down from the Valleys a year or two back when she'd married young Stan George the fireman. She'd been his Double-home landlady's daughter at Llandeilo—he hadn't stood a chance, man—it was up to the altar in six months and a christening seven months later. But he hadn't done too badly—quite a pretty little thing she was really, in a dark, Celtic sort of way. Although I know for a fact that Dai had left his ladder in their back garden on at least three occasions when Stan was on the Late Goods. Not that that proves anything, mind. He often left it over at Dago Jones' place or at old Miss Post Office Davies's. Skilful he was—bloody skilful, fair play.

The unmistakable highly pungent aroma from the Boys' open air latrine wafted gently across the hot playground to my twitching nostrils as I mounted the steps to the narrow double doors and carefully manipulated my ladder beneath the engraved coping stone. ''Llanporth Board School 1871'', and I smiled to myself as I recalled how, for years as a kid, I'd thought that the figures stood for the address—*The School, 1,871 High Street, Llanporth!* Seeing nothing incongrous in the fact that we lived not many doors away and that our number was only 32!

Nothing had changed over the years. There was still that same musty smell of stale ink, old books and sweaty clothes which had struck sickening terror into my heart the very first day I had stepped reluctantly over the threshold to encounter the grim, black-sateened figure of old Miss Slatter. The next to last peg in the narrow hallway was still broken off and. the dust-laden, trailing cobwebs still hung disinterestedly down from the dark, high corners, the box of jam jars still stood in the corner and the coloured bands for Physical Training still hung from their special nail on the back of the Babies' Classroom door.

Mam had had to prize open every one of my fear-damp fingers in order to free her hand which I'd held onto with such grim tenacity that never forgotten day of 1900; then my greaseproof-wrapped, cold toast for my first playtime had been greedily snatched away by a grinning giant from Standard Six and I had made up my mind to run away to sea after dinner rather than return to this house of strangers. I'd always been told, in a tone of mixed admiration and condemnation, that Granfer Davies had run away to sea when he was a boy, so it had seemed the only solution for me too. But I never did get round to it!

Carefully negotiating my way along the narrow coat-hook decorated passage way, I leant the ladder up against the wall, opened the door in the glass partition and poked my head inquiringly round the corner.

"Just come to mend the hinges," I explained as a sea of faces swung round to stare at me. For a brief moment I failed to pinpoint the teacher anywhere, when suddenly the lovely fragrance of Lily of the Valley jostled with the stale smell of perspiring bodies and from behind the door came a delightful apparition of cool, slim loveliness.

"*Uffern dân!*" I thought taken aback. I'd forgotten a new school mistress had started that week—old Miss Slatter having finally agreed to be pensioned off at the age of seventy-two.

"Oh, do come in," she welcomed and a ravishing smile spread across her delicate features. "Mr. Dai Rees, isn't it? Mr. Jenkins told me to expect you."

I was about to assure her, in a delirious, fleeting moment of madness, that I was Dai Rees, with fantastic visions of re-found freedom of pursuit and dalliance flashing in my brain, when I heard myself stammering, "No, Miss . . . no, Evan Evans, I am . . . helping out." Well, she was bound to have found out soon, anyway! "Er . . . Mr. Rees isn't feeling up to it this afternoon—he has these spasms . . . you know . . ." and I gave a knowing nod of the head and she gave a knowing nod of sympathetic understanding back! Well, he needed handicapping a bit, after all, to give the rest of us a chance! But

I couldn't help wishing that I hadn't put Dai's scruffy pair of overalls on that particular afternoon. My second best blue serge and panama hat would have made a far better impression I felt sure.

''All right if I put this by 'ere, Miss . . . er . . . Miss . . .?''

"Miss Thomas," she volunteered," yes, that'll be all right.''

I dumped my tool frail on an empty desk in the front row, stepped back and viewed the hinges of the partition with a professional air.

"It's the one at the top, Mr. Evans," she said helpfully, coming close to my shoulder to point out the offending hinge.

"Which one?" I questioned, although I could see it damn well, but it meant that this angel of delight would stay at my side for a bit longer, directing my gaze with an elegant finger. There's lovely her perfume was—even better than Ruby Tyler's California Poppy.

''Right you are, Miss Thomas, I'll have that fixed for you in no time at all,''I promised with one of my best smiles and managing to make it sound as if I was doing her a personal favour.

There hadn't been a sound from the class, so intrigued they'd been with this novel interruption to the afternoon's routine, except for a lone slate pencil busily squeaking away, its industrious owner lost in the absorbing task of practising loops on his letters ready for double writing in The Big Class. I glanced round at the room as I went to fetch the ladder from the passageway. It was far smaller and more cramped than I had remembered.

The little ones, staring at me with great interest, sat at their scarred and stained desks with tangled balls of G.W.R. cotton waste in front of them, from which they had been meticulously sorting the different coloured strands of cotton into neat little piles. I'd swear they were the same damn balls of waste we'd used twenty years before. I often wondered why we'd spent hour after hour sorting each tiny coloured thread—only to see old Miss Slatter tangle them all up again at the end of each lesson! Mind you, I won't say I didn't enjoy it at the time. Nice and peaceful it was at the end of a long day's work, and satisfying too, achieving order out of chaos I suppose.

I'd never realised before how embarrassingly incongruous

the older backward boys and girls looked in this Infants' classroom. There they sat at the back of the room, as they'd always done, their slates and pencils before them, their knees poking out awkwardly on either side of the too low desks as they resignedly endeavoured to wedge themselves into the ill-fitting Infants' furniture. Four boys and one girl there were, with Dull Reggie, beetroot faced and perspiring, encased in his bristling dark green jersey and heavy, crumpled grey jacket, looking even more clumsy and lumbering than usual in contrast to the little infants around him.

But fair play, only two classrooms there were, and as old Jenkins pointed out, you can't have them slowing down all the rest of them, now can you? He took the brighter, older children himself, on the other side of the partition, coaching hard every Spring for the Scholarship, and the following September his efforts were rewarded by two or three star pupils winning places at the County School. The remainder, meanwhile, simply returned to Llanporth Board School to do the same work again the following year . . . and the next . . . and the next . . . until they could legally finish their education and thankfully leave. Both Dai and I had managed to pass the Scholarship, but we didn't stay at the County school long enough to take our C.W.B.—so we left at fourteen, but I can still remember a bit of French—only a few words mind, and one sentence in Latin—'discipuli picturam spectate', which were the first words in the book., 'Children look at the picture' it means—I think. So it was worth while going to The County, I suppose, after all.

But the real dull ones who had to stay down with the Infants simply passed the endless, chalk dust years forever tidying up, being 'monitors', doing odd jobs and occasionally trying to wrestle with the intricacies and bewildering difficulties of learning to Read, Write and Do Sums. Poor dabs. But they had a few special privileges, fair play. They were allowed to dig and weed old Jenkins' garden for him and run errands for Mrs. Jenkins. And, if they were lucky, they were chosen to paint his fence every spring and help beat the carpets. So they didn't do too badly really—considering. Occasionally things went a bit wrong mind—like the time Shandy Lewis planted old Jenkins' onions in artistic half-moons in the front garden instead of his daffodil bulbs and then followed it up with meticulously taking all the eyes out of his seed potatoes with his cherished clasp knife, before planting them next to the daffodils in the plot at the back! Dull as a bat he was—never got past Standard Two, but he seemed to be coping all right now, looking after Rees the Farm's cows. That's the way it goes, isn't it? We all find a niche somewhere, and by the time you're married and got a few kiddies, what does it matter that you never learnt your tables and couldn't spell—bugger all it matters.

So I gave Dull Regie a broad wink and a nod of encouragement before I disappeared out into the passage, where I was almost bowled over by a desperate six year old, frantically pushing past me as he made his bee-line for the outside lavatory. There was no mistaking that palpable, crutch-clutched haste—the damp memory of my own last minute dashes for relief were still all too vivid—and still are—especially the one humiliating occasion when, engrossed in putting the finishing touches to a carrot I was painting in Standard One, I became aware of a hot trickle running down to my socks and found myself, to my horror, sitting on a flooded seat overflowing with copious splashings onto the floor beneath. Damn, there's shame I felt—with Miss Slatter's poky finger pointing accusingly under my chair for everyone to see and the big boys giggling behind their hands while I walked, ignomineously straddle legged to fetch a mop and bucket. Stinging red-raw the tops of my legs were by the time I got home at four o'clock, with the wet, rough worsted cloth chaffing at them. I can't really say that I've been too fond of carrots ever since!

"Back to work, children," remonstrated the enchanting Miss Thomas as I banged my way a bit awkwardly through the door with Dai's ladder. "Mr. Evans doesn't want you watching everything he does, I'm sure."

No, but I wouldn't mind you watching, my lovely, I thought, as I climbed purposefully up to the broken hinge. I gave the screws a bit of a tap with the hammer to loosen them a bit before starting to unscrew them, taking surreptitious glances down at the fluffy haze of golden hair below me. Definitely League One, I reckoned, as I mentally stripped her down to her lovely fair skin and slowly proceeded to dress her again from scratch in all the most delicious items from the First League shelves in the shop. Dai would be tamping mad when he found out what an opportunity he missed just to put his damn old posts in. Really rub it in, I would.

Fancy discovering two new members for the First League in one afternoon, I marvelled. Things were definitely looking up in Llanporth, and the sooner I put those models in the window the better, I decided as I wrestled with one particularly stubborn screw. Put in in 1871 and had no intention of coming out now, by the feel of it neither. The clangour of the handbell in old Jenkins' room interrupted my mental and physical exertions, both of which were, by this time, making me feel bloody hot, I can tell you. A sigh of relief rose from the youngsters below me, the heavy tip-up seats clanked up as they shuffled to their feet, put their hands together, closed their eyes and automatically started to chant the four o'clock prayer . . . 'Dear Lord, keep us safe this night, until tomorrow's morning light. A . . . men.' Eyes squinted up at me through grubby clasped fingers as the mechanically uttered, sing-song words echoed through the high classroom. There was a second's pause of fidgety silence before Miss Thomas announced 'Hands down . . . Side step' and the class obediently side-stepped out into the aisles, stood to attention and tramped out to the command 'Forwarch March'.

The air outside was immediately rent with raucous cheering, shouting and the clatter of boots as the children were let loose from the school regime and I recalled how thoroughly we'd appreciated the four o'clock freedom. The village would be coming splendidly alive now as the forty or more youngsters charged their way through the school gate, filling the streets with their excited chatter, laughter and quarrels. Mams would be moving the blackened kettles off the hob onto the fire and slicing mountains of bread and butter and jam ready to satisfy the ravenous appetites and Dull Reggie's younger sister, her sacking pinny rolled under her arm, would be making her slow way to The Prince Albert to scrub out the bar, and clean the spitoons.

I put my shoulder behind the screwdriver with renewed determination and this time my efforts were rewarded as the obstinate screw finally relinqished its staunch grip of over half a century and submissively spiralled its way out of its wooden matrix, all the fight gone out of it as it acknowledged me as master. The classroom lay unaccustomedly quiet and still. The industrious mental activity of the day had suddenly ceased leaving only shimmering particles of chalk dust glinting in the sun's rays streaming in through the high windows and spit-wiped slates rapidly drying on the deserted desks.

"Aren't you hot with your jersey and coat on, Reggie?" came a quiet voice. I looked down in some surprise, having assumed that all the children had left in the mass exodus a few minutes before; Dull Reggie looked up from the pile of books he was tidying up on the shelves behind the blackboard and easel.

"No Miss," he mumbled, his face beetroot red, his dark hair sticking damply to his glistening forehead as he pulled his coat protectingly round his chest and carefully did up the one and only button.

"It's very warm today—why don't you take them off for a little while—you'll feel much cooler," the coaxing voice went on.

Reggie slowly stopped tidying up the books and stared undecidedly down at his boots as his lovely Miss Thomas cleared the day's clutter from the top of her high desk. After a few seconds of tortured indecision spent examining his polish-starved boots, Reggie took a deep breath, undid his button and reluctantly started to wriggle his way out of his heavy, shapeless jacket, carefully re-arranging his slipped braces over his shoulders before presenting himself for a word of praise from his beloved 'Miss'—well—it was obvious that he worshipped her, and who could blame him? He was a fraction taller than she was and twice as heavy, his clumsy hands hanging loosely at his side as usual as he waited patiently for her to turn and give him a smile of approval.

There's different from old Miss Slatter—big, vicious crosses and grudging little ticks she used to mark all over our work. I'd bet anything that this fair-haired beauty gave tiny little crosses and lovely big ticks. She turned to her lumbering admirer.

"Well done, Reggie!" she commended, smiling up at his broad, dirty face and he beamed back happily, obviously delighted to have done something right.

"Can you remember your reading today?" she went on. Reggie furrowed his brow with concentration as his teacher picked up a piece of chalk and wrote 'I must work hard' on the blackboard. He stared at the meaningless jumble of letters,

41

screwing up his velvet brown, thick lashed eyes as he waited for inspiration. Poor bugger, I thought, how the hell does he manage to keep so bloody happy.

"I . . . must . . . " she coaxed.

"I must," repeated Reggie hopefully.

"I must work . . ." she repeated and I could almost see her willing him to remember.

Suddenly Reggie's flash of inspiration came. Up shot his hand in delight. "I must work hard!" he announced triumphantly, almost hugging himself with glee.

"Well done, Reggie, well done!" came the longed for praise and Dull Reggie's face was a picture of happiness. "Now off you go home and I'll see you again tomorrow," Miss Thomas added with another of her smiles.

"I took my coat off, Miss," he reminded her, again.

"I'm very glad," she approved, "Now, off you go." Reluctantly he ambled his way to the door, looked up curiously at me atop my ladder, concentrated hard as he obviously tried to think where he'd seen me before, gave up and disappeared out into the passageway.

Poor bugger, I though for the second time, as if he didn't have enough to contend with without me doing a Jekyll and Hyde on him to confuse him even further.

I watched him dawdle his lonely way across the empty playground, knowing that by the morning he would sadly have forgotten everything again.

But he didn't know he was lonely. He didn't know that he forgot everything he was told. Each new day was a separate existence and tomorrow he'd be happily re-born again, with 'I must work hard' floating only vaguely through his mindless subconscious like a shadowy, pre-natal dream.

"You've got a job on there, love," I commented with sympathy as I chiselled away a few slivers of wood to fit the new hinge snugly in place.

"Poor old Reggie," she agreed with a despairing shake of the head, taking no umbrage, I was pleased to note, at being addressed as 'love'. 'Miss Thomas' it would have to have been if I'd been Dressed for Drapery, mind. 'Love' would have sounded a bit familiar in blue serge and a collar and tie, but it was quite acceptable from Dai's overalls. Very subtle these things, but it made the difference between success and utter failure where the ladies were concerned, as I'd learnt very early in my existence.

"Nearly finished?" Old Jenkins deep voice rumbled from his jowls as he came in and stared up at me.

"Ten minutes and it'll be done," I assured him, "Nasty little job it was," I added, not wanting it to appear too simple a task and thinking of Dai's bill.

He turned away and rolled heavily across the room towards the sylphlike figure who was wiping off the momentous words from the blackboard. "Ah . . . Miss Thomas, I was wondering if you would like to come along to our Choir Practice this evening," and he rocked dangerously back on his heels as he fingered the gold watch chain stretched across the wide expanse of stomach.

Bloody good show! I thought with delight, nearly falling off the ladder as the screwdriver slipped out of the slot of the screw in my excitement.

"Well, I've never done much singing, Mr. Jenkins," she demured. "I don't think I sing very well, really,"

Who cares if you can sing, my lovely, I thought to myself, just you come and stand there, that's all we want.

"'Course you can sing . . . seven o'clock at the Baptist Schoolroom then?" Old Jenkins brushed aside her hesitation with a headmaster's air of authority and strode largely out of the room.

"Ahm . . . I go to Choir," I volunteered, "I'll look after you, don't you worry." and I gave her a reassuring smile.

"I'll see you there, then," she agreed as she placed a wide floppy brimmed hat on top of her blonde curls, gave me a wave and disappeared through the door, leaving a faint fragrance of her Lily of the Valley filtering up to the beams and my appreciative nostrils as I vowed to wear a clean shirt and my new Come-to-Jesus cut-away collar to Choir Practice that night.

*   *   *

"Been a lovely day, Mr. Evans."

Guiltily I flicked my braces back up over my shoulders as the lilting young voice caught me by surprise. Myra was always telling me off for getting myself ready on my way down the path to the lav at the bottom of the garden. But old habits die hard, and with only old Ernie living next door for donkeys years there had been no need to delay proceedings until the Tŷ Bach had been actually reached. But now that young Susie Webb and her new husband had moved in, I reluctantly had to agree with Myra that I would have to try to remember to be a bit more circumspect.

"Lovely, indeed," I agreed, looking up at the hazy blue sky for confirmation. "Alan on the early then, this week?" I queried, just to pass the time.

"Working the 12.15 from Cardiff, he is—should be home soon," she smiled and went on picking the soft blackberries, over-ripened against the warm stone wall.

I gave a nod for the information and continued on my errand of nature, carefully closing the latch of the Tŷ Bach behind me and giving it a gentle rattle to test its efficiency. Well, it was a bit worn and I didn't want the damn door drifting open half way through after all, not with young Susie just the other side of the low stone wall.

I swatted a few flies with my newspaper before settling myself down with pleasurable anticipation to indulge in a good old read by the dim light from the circular vent holes drilled in the door. I'd decided not to say a word to Dai about the new school mistress, when I'd returned his ladder and tools. Instead I was relishing the look on his face when this gorgeous stranger turned up at Choir Practice and he discovered that I was already well in. Mad he'd be then about not going up to the school himself.

Time drifted by un-noticed as I contentedly rustled my way through the news, when my reverie was disturbed by a small shriek just outside.

"Got you my lovely!" a deep voice growled quietly and the squeal changed to a feminine giggle of delight. Young Alan was home by the sound of it, I thought with a grin. It was just about time he got married too—give somebody else a chance behind the Cricket Club up on the Common—beginning to think he owned that patch he was. But Susie had caught him and up to the altar at Bethesda he'd marched that Spring, just a week after old Ernie had paid his last visit there in one of Dai's second class coffins. Very considerate of him to die just then, really, for as soon as his furniture was sold up, Alan and Susie rented No. 34 and moved in.

The gruff whispers and giggles went on as I sat on the warm wooden seat, smiling to myself.

"Oh . . . mind Alan . . . the neighbours'll see . . ."

"Bugger the neighbours!" came the low growl.

"But I've got to clean the shallots for tea . . ."

"Bugger my tea!" The whisper reached my ears through the cobwebbed ventholes and then there was silence . . .

Mindful of Myra's warning, I re-arranged my braces and checked all my buttons before lifting the latch and stepping out once more into the late afternoon sunshine. But my caution was wasted—the next door garden was deserted, the basin of blackberries stood forgotten on the path and the pulled shallots, their fleshy roots shrinking as they dried in the warm sunshine, lay wilting on the wall next to an oil stained G.W.R. cap.

"Randy bugger!" I thought with a grin as I viewed the empty garden, the abandoned blackberries and discarded cap—wait till I see him at Choir—I'd pull his leg for him! I always thought that taking your cap off was the second thing you were supposed to do!

But as I reached the kitchen door I felt the amused grin fade from my lips and a worrying idea started to niggle inside my head . . . was I as randy as that? In fact, was I ever as randy as that? I mean, he hadn't even waited until he'd had his tea! Damn good you are at the chatting up, Evan Evans, I told myself but when it comes down to brass tacks . . . I blanched at the admission. "Rubbish" I muttered angrily. I pulled back my shoulders and put my hand firmly on the latch. I'll show 'em, I thought, I'll show 'em I'm not all bloody talk! I'm as randy as the next man! Don't you worry!

"Myra!" I called as I stepped in through the door. "Where are you, love?"

But even before she answered I was having second thoughts. After all, I reasoned, Choir Practice was in just over half an hour's time, and quite strenuous it was singing under Old Cy—and I wanted to be on top form . . .

"Did you want me, Evan?" Myra popped her head round the passage door, her eyebrows raised.

"Er . . . yes . . . love . . . What about . . . what about another cup of tea before Choir?"

Chapter 3

Fred Harris the Signalman and his young brother Steve, their fiery red heads close together in the far corner of the crowded Baptist Schoolroom, were gently experimenting with the tenor line of 'O Lord, thou hast overthrown', while I kept my eyes peeled on the door for the first glimpse of Ann Thomas. I'd discovered her christian name from Myra, who had learnt it from Mrs. Know-all Jones when she'd come into the shop for a bit of a gossip that very afternoon. Lodging with the two Miss Tugwells behind their bun and cake shop, she was, so Myra had found out, although nobody had seen much of her as yet . . . except me, I'd thought smugly.

'We'll knock'em cold with this one," remarked Cy Lloyd the Butcher confidently as he handed me my Elijah copy, referring to the Martletwy Eisteddfod coming up in six weeks time. "Great recitatives it's got." Cy always liked to include a piece with a bit of recitative in it so that we could show off Umshla's fine tenor or Jenkins' noble bass, and 'O Lord, thou hast overthrown' had a bit for both of them, so our hopes were really high. The Set Piece, this year was "Ere to dust is changed thy beauty" and Cy had picked our Free Choice pieces very carefully. His well-tried recipe for success was to choose one with a recitative, one slow, melancholy piece in a minor key so that our sweet, lingering harmony could wring tears from the eyes of the most hardened adjudicator, and one to finish with a roof-raising chorus full of rousing Allelujahs and glorious long Amens to leave the hall ringing as his baton brought us to a splendid finale,—although he did try to avoid any piece with sharps in it, because F sharp wouldn't play on the Baptist piano and Miss Davies said it put her off having a cluck note and her accompaniment went all hay-wire. But she had to put up with it sometimes, although you could tell she didn't like it one little bit.

"Where the hell are Frankie Evans and Old Lloyd got to?" grumbled Cy, scanning the room for our missing double basses. "They've had plenty of time to lubricate their damn tubes by now, surely," he pointed out, confirming, with a vexed look at his pocket watch, that it was half an hour past opening time at The Prince Albert. "D flat, Miss Davies, D flat!" he commented a bit irritably as poor Miss Davies struggled discordantly with the four flats of 'O Lord, Thou hast overthrown'.

"But there's something wrong with the piano, Mr. Lloyd," she apologised timidly.

"Aw Gawd!" he breathed at me in despair, raising his eyes to the ceiling and walking off to hand out a few more copies.

"'Evening Mr. Evans," came a low, succulent voice from behind my shoulder. No need to guess who it was—that heady California Poppy was already contesting the vestige of fishpaste and cucumber sandwiches which was lingering on the Chapel air from the Women's Institute tea that afternoon.

"Very formal, aren't we?" I whispered back, not taking my eyes off my choral copy.

"In public, we are, aren't we?" came the equally quiet reply, and smiling brightly over at the sopranos, Mrs. Ruby Tyler stood by my side.

"Proper dandy you're looking this evening, aren't you?" she commented, eyeing my new two-tone shoes and cutaway collar in some surprise. "Who are you out to impress, then?" and she viewed the assembled group of chattering, humming, throat-clearing songsters for a suitable feminine object of my attentions. Too bloody astute she was, by half, that's a fact, I thought.

"Me, is it?" she asked archly, raising her thinly pencilled eyebrows in an ingenuous look of surprise. And I gave her what I hoped was an intimate smile—well, what else could I do! Better than saying no wasn't it? And she did look bloody lovely.

"Matthew had to go to some old Customs and Excise meeting at Fishguard this afternoon," she remarked casually, giving a nod and a wave over to the contraltos. "Stopping with his cousin in Lower Town tonight, he is . . ." and she looked curiously up at me to watch the reaction on my face to this momentous piece of news.

I cleared my throat and hastily turned over two pages of my choral copy.

"Oh." I said, inadequately, suddenly conscious of my little toe stinging with the unaccustomed, tight pressure of my new two-tones.

"Dare say you could do with a cup of tea after Choir, Mr. Evans," she went on, emphasising the Mister with a smile.

47

"I've left the kettle on the hob if you fancy calling in . . ."

There it was—in my lap—just like that. After all this time. Three years I'd spent chatting her up, ever since they'd moved into The Customs House from Haverfordwest, but I'd never imagined that it would actually lead anywhere. A host of scenes flashed through my mind, from lazily, half-closed eyes looking invitingly over the rim of a cup of tea to a full-scale seduction on her front parlour mat, rapidly followed by the vivid picture of her neighbour, Mrs. Know-all Jones calling in at the shop the following day for a 'chat' with Myra. My hands went clammy and sweat started to trickle down the small of my back at the thought.

Good God, what am I going to do? I thought. Somebody might see me going in—or worse still—coming out! No doubt about it, she'd called my bluff good and proper—although I wasn't really bluffing, I tried to convince myself, it was just that the circumstances were a bit too tricky. But how was I going to get out of it without losing too much face? *Uffern dân!* I'd never live it down if ever Dai found out about it.

I cleared my throat again and looked down at the slightly amused smile on the tantalising face at my side, when suddenly a feeling of relief flooded through me . . . my models!

"Damn and blast!" I swore fervently under my breath, managing to sound furious instead of relieved, "I've got to go and collect some goods from the railway sidings after Choir. Why did that damn husband of yours have to go and choose this very night to stop in Fishguard?" I whispered irately, managing to make my voice sound full of unrequited passion—although, to tell the truth, I was feeling a bit jaded—well, it had been an exhausting day after all, fair play, "I've simply got to fetch the damn things," I explained, ruefully, as her beautiful face clouded for a second, "otherwise they'll be off back to Cardiff! And I've got Dai Rees's handtruck outside all ready and waiting."

"Well," she said brightly, with a slight shrug of her elegant shoulders, "You know you're always welcome for a cup of tea anytime, Mr. Evans," and off she sauntered without a backward glance, leaving me limp with relief—well, too risky it would have been, after all. Funny, but Ruby was one of the few ladies who didn't fancy Dai—never gave him a second glance—just like Myra. At least, I didn't think Myra fancied him, although, on reflection she always made apple pie specially without cloves whenever he came to dinner—and she knew I loved cloves. I'd have to watch him, I resolved with some apprehension. Never short of a good dinner was Dai—wherever he happened to be working the lady of the house always took it upon herself to cook him a fine meal. Twenty per cent sympathy for his living on his own since his Mam and Pa died within six months of each other two years back and eighty per cent feminine wiles it was . . . "Look at my Dilys (or Megan or Mair, etc) by there—not yet nineteen and as good a cook as her Mam any day, aren't you my lovely?" And the thick juicy slices of rabbit pie would be put on the table for Dai's appreciative palate. Loved good eating he did, but loved his freedom more—be blowed, he did! Well, everyone knew his Pa had left him quite comfortably off, six hundred he'd had at least, apart from the hundred and fifty he'd had from his old Aunt Cis in Llanstephan, so quite a catch Dai would be for some lucky girl, but she'd have to be pretty smart, I can tell you.

The jarring discord of another missed D flat brought my wandering thoughts back to the dusty Chapel Schoolroom and to poor old Miss Davies who was complaining most plaintively to anyone who cared to listen that top G simply would not play tonight, and she couldn't be expected to give of her best with an F sharp and a G gone cluck right next to each other, and the loud pedal had gone floppy again and Mr. Lloyd would be so cross if she couldn't hold on to the semibreves in the recitative.

Poor dab, I thought, fancy being a League Four and having to cope with a floppy loud pedal to boot.

"Can I help you, Miss Davies?" I asked most solicitously.

"Oh, thank you Mr. Evans, you're so kind—do you think you could find Mr. Dai Rees—he's mended the piano before and he is so very clever . . ." And she smiled gratefully up at me. Well, damn me—even old Miss Davies was turning me down for Dai now, I thought with a grin as I turned to find him.

"Dai!" I yelled over the laughter, chat and experimental singing, "Bit of repair for you," I beckoned as soon as I caught his eye. Right in the middle of the contraltos he was—trust him.

"What's the matter, love?" he asked, leaning over the top of the piano and beaming down at the worried Miss Davies. Gwendoline Davies was forty if she was a day—a confirmed 'spinster of this parish', but Dai could get away with murder the things he said to her. Very prim she was with everybody else, but Dai pulled her leg and chatted her up with such utter disregard for her droopy crocheted jumper, her equally droopy uneven-hemmed skirt, her tightly knotted bun and disapproving look, that she came over all flustered and girlish—loved it she did!

"Your candlesticks got stuck, then?" he joked, giving them a quick flick back and fore across the propped sheet of music.

"Oh, Mr. Rees," she twittered, her bony hand clasped across her flat bosom, "No, no, it's my top G," and she prodded it ineffectively with her forefinger, "and my pedal has gone floppy again."

"Nasty that!" he commented with a grin across at me. "Well, shove over then, love, and I'll see what I can do," and under the piano Dai delved, taking a screwdriver out of his back pocket. "Damn thing's worked loose again," he announced with a grunt, which was no wonder really the amount of travelling it did—well, it wasn't every practice we could have in the Baptist Schoolroom—superceded we were sometimes by Prayer Meetings, Parish Council meetings, Young Folk's Knitting and Sewing Classes and other parochial activities—then down to Cy's Abattoir we'd have to trundle the piano, but I reckon it was the two steps leading up to the slaughterhouse behind the shop that did the damage. Mind you, the Baptists weren't too keen on our shifting it about, but as it had been left to them by old Perkins' widow (a fine bass old Perkins had been) on the understanding that it was available at anytime for Choir Practices, they couldn't very well refuse.

"Try it now then, love—put your little foot on it by there and see if it goes," and Dai heaved himself from under the keyboard and patted Gwendoline's well-covered knee affectionately.

"Oh, Mr. Rees, you are clever," she flustered, her cheeks scarlet at the unaccustomed attention. "I'll give it a real test," she announced, and positioned her hands over the keys, played a chord and lifted her fingers off with a flourish. The jangle of almost-in-tune notes continued to reverberate on and she

50

beamed with delight. "Oh, you are clever!" she repeated and blushed even more furiously.

"Now, what's the matter with your blessed top G?" he went on, opening the lid and peering into the works. Miss Davies struck the silent offending note accusingly with her finger, when suddenly it started to ring out and from the dark innards Dai produced a small square of half unravelled knitting!

"Well, I never!" Miss Davies marvelled.

"All part of the service, girl—you know I'd do anything for you," and he gave a sweeping bow, pocketed his screwdriver and was about to make his way back to his contraltos when he stopped dead in his tracks.

"Hey, boy," he breathed, with a hefty nudge in my ribs, "Look at what's just walked in . . . who the bloody hell is that then?" I followed his slightly stunned gaze to the door, where, standing beneath the scroll of past Women's Institute Presidents, was the slim, enchanting figure of Ann Thomas, looking a little hesitant as she searched for a familiar face.

"Oh," I remarked casually, "that's Ann," making it sound as if we were really well acquainted. "Ann Thomas, the new mistress up at the school. Nice girl she is—very friendly."

"You mean you met her this afternoon," he stared at me in disbelief, "while I was hammering those damn posts in the field!" Real vexed he was, I could tell.

"I arranged to meet her here tonight, so I'd better pop over to say hello," and off I sauntered with a friendly wave in her direction as I caught her eye, conscious of a flabbergasted Dai staring at my back.

"Hello, Mr. Evans, I didn't recognise you at first," she greeted with a smile, Damn me, I thought as I automatically fingered my Come-to-Jesus cut-away collar, she was even more lovely than I remembered, standing there in a little sailor-suit dress and pale stockings.

"Call me Evan—it's my christian name as well, you see," I hastened to explain as she looked a little puzzled.

"Oh, I see," she laughed. "My name is Ann."

"Aren't you going to introduce me then?" came a voice at my side and I knew that Dai had abandoned all thoughts of returning to his contraltos. Never wasted a second, he did.

"Miss Thomas—this is Mr. Dai Rees," I explained a little

reluctantly, while Dai put on his most charming smile and shook her hand with lingering, warm approval.

"Are you feeling better, Mr. Rees?" she enquired solicitously, "Evan, here, said you weren't feeling too well this afternoon . . ."

Dai looked taken aback for a moment, then glared daggers at me, but I was busy perusing my choral copy and humming a few bars.

"I expect it's a bit dangerous going up a ladder if you're not feeling quite . . . mh . . . quite right." she added.

"Why no—there was nothing wrong with me," he hastened to explain, "Never had a day's illness in my life. Just a bit busy, I was, that was all."

I gave an unseen warning frown from behind his back and Ann gave an imperceptible nod of consideration, fully grasping that if Dai didn't want to talk about his 'spasms', she quite understood!

Dai suddenly turned to me with a matey smile, "How's the wife then?" he asked with great deliberation and a vengeful gleam in his eye. Well, that made us quits, I thought ruefully as I made some casual reply. Sometimes I couldn't make up my mind if he was my best friend or my worst enemy—always been the same!

Further conversation was halted by Cy Lloyd hurrying over, hand outstretched to greet the new member of his Choir.

"Welcome, Miss Thomas, to the Llanporth Choral Group. Mr. Jenkins told me you'd be joining us. Delighted we are to gain a new voice—aren't we friends?" he asked, his gaze encompassing the gathered throng, and a murmur of assent and approval rustled through the room as he swept her off for the numerous introductions.

"You knew she'd be here, didn't you?" and there was Ruby eyeing me with a dawning look of enlightenment.

"Now, how the devil would I know a thing like that?" I replied, open eyed with innocence. She looked down deliberately at my shoes and up at my Come-to-Jesus collar, stared me in the eye and mouthed "Liar!" and walked off. *Uffarn Dân!* I thought, I hoped I wasn't going to have trouble there—and they were both sopranos too.

Frank Evans the Guard and Lloyd the Stationmaster, having suitably lubricated their tubes, came strolling in to join us at that moment, the latter accompanied by his customary semi-suppressed burp—about one every half hour came rumbling up from the depths throughout each day without fail, no doubt various flavours, mind, but it was a bit of a nuisance if one chose to bubble to the surface right in the middle of a bit of somebody's solo recitative. Cy, in desperation, had suggested that he tried to have one just before it began, but old Lloyd maintained that it wasn't as easy as that. "You can't interfere with Nature," he'd point out reasonably, "It's nothing to do with me," disclaiming all responsibility for his stomach's explosive tendency.

"Everything arranged for tonight?" Frank Evans whispered anxiously in my ear.

"Don't worry, it's all under control," I assured him.

"Good. Good." He repeated with a sigh of relief. "It's just that Mrs. Evans . . . you know . . ." and off he hurried to get a copy of 'O, Lord, Thou hast overthrown'.

The sharp tapping as Cy rapped his conductor's baton on the music stand brought Miss Davies's feverish last minute practice to an abrupt mid-bar halt while the rest of us shuffled about to take up our correct places.

"We'll skip the recitative for now and go straight into the chorus." Cy instructed.

Mrs. L. Y. T. Jones (League 3½) adjusted her lace modesty vest over the plunging neckline dipping bravely down between her vast bosom; the tenors noisily cleared their throats; Mrs. Ruby Tyler glanced casually at her music copy; Alf the Lion, in anticipation of having to hang on to a B flat for fifteen beats towards the end of 'Thanks be to God', surreptitiously removed his top set and slipped the gleaming, grinning dentures into his back pocket, having, as they did, the unfortunate tendency to drop down with a resounding sharp click if he had to keep his mouth wide open for too long; Davis the Coal took a swift nip from his hip flask; Dai positioned himself in the front line of tenors, right behind Ann Thomas—the bugger; I winced as another shooting pain shot through my tightly compressed little toe; the sopranos poised themselves with raised shoulders and inflated lungs; Lloyd the Stationmaster was taken by surprise by a premature burp arriving ten minutes early and we all launched ourselves into the close harmony of 'Open the heavens and send us relief: Help, help, thy servant now, O God!'

Choir Practice was under way.

*   *   *

A thunderous twilight hung heavily over the High Street as the exhausted, throat-parched members of the Llanporth Choir slowly filtered past Dull Reggie who was in his usual listening corner of the dark little vestibule, and out on to the narrow pavement, the triumphant Allelujahs and Amens of 'Zadock The Priest' still ringing in our ears. Miss Gwendoline Davies, who hadn't had too successful an evening, poor dab, scuttled off down the hill, the heavy, spare key to the Baptist Schoolroom clutched in her hand so that she could let herself in to get a bit of extra practice before the following week. Well, semiquaver runs weren't her forte at the best of times and she usually relied on our choral output to cover up any missing notes. The trouble was that Zadock's 'God Save the King' had quite a few solo runs for the piano and even when the choir came in it was often short staccato and poor Gwendoline's fumbled semiquavers showed up with devastating clarity.

"Try and sort 'em out by next week, Miss Davies, there's a good girl," Cy had pleaded when she'd ended up half a bar behind our Amen for the third time in succession. But as there were the notorious F sharps in it, none of us held out too much hope for any dramatic improvement. But fair play, she was great on chords and had managed to give us a grand opening, the loud pedal squeaking up and down with the panache of a true professional, so you couldn't grumble too much—besides, there was no-one else available-except Dai Bach Chips, and he only played by ear, which didn't really do justice to Handel, and, on the few occasions when he obliged because Miss Davies was poorly, he nearly drove a frantic Cy to despair as he never played the same version twice.

"Threat of thunder about, I reckon," observed Frank as we stood under the yellow pool of gas light outside the Bethesda holding our usual post mortem on the standard of the performance at the Practice . . .

"Well, if the tenors had held on, as they should have done . . ."

"Two beats too soon you came in . . ."

"Couldn't hear the damn contraltos . . ."

"You've got to count, see . . . got to count . . ."

". . . no point in a diminuendo if we don't all do it . . ."

Exactly the same enjoyable procedure it was every Thursday night outside the British Legion Hut after the Whistdrive. The tone of voice, the shrug of shoulder, the righteous accusation, they were just the same—only the subject differed . . .

". . . if you'd led a Heart instead of that Diamond . . ."

". . . only took three tricks with seven trumps, mind . . ."

". . . well, everyone knew that the Ace had gone . . ."

". . . I only played the Queen because I thought you had the . . ."

Real disappointing it was, if it was raining and we had to fore-go our post mortems and hurry home. Seemed to have missed half the pleasure, somehow.

"Concentrate on the Zadock this week, then, Umshla," instructed Cy, referring to Umshla's unofficial Practices with any G.W.R. tenors he could round up into his conveniently placed carriage shunted into the local siding. I often popped in to join them myself, if I happened to hear the strains of a bit of Elijah, Messiah or Zadock filtering through the clatter and noise of the shunting locos. Well, it all helped and it was amazing how much we improved, sitting there, in the Third Class Compartment side by side on the dusty moquette seats, the air heavy with the sulphurous haze emanating from the overall-clad, duty-mitching G.W.R. tenors. Put a copy of a piece of music in Umshla's hands and he was away, boy, no hesitation. Real confident. Over and over we'd sing the tricky passages, under his expert guidance until the Practice was inevitably broken up by young Steve Harris the Fireman apologetically explaining that if he didn't go and get steam up for the 4.20 Goods, his Driver would half kill him—or some such Railway Requisite ranging from locos needing cleaning to empties needing shunting. "B.B.B.B.B. . .Bl. . .Blooming nuisance. . ." Umshla would mutter, resignedly gathering up the grimy-finger marked copies. "S. . .S. . .same. . .same. . . same t. . .t. . .time, tomorrow. . ." he'd remind us with a wagging finger and off he'd go back to his weeding, his Porter's cap regulation-straight a-top his head, his sheaf of music tucked under his arm. Very particular he was about his uniform, well, after all, he was proud to be working for the G.W.R . . .!

I looked round surreptitiously for any glimpse of Ann Thomas or Mrs. Ruby Tyler, but both were hemmed in by a bevy of sopranos and contraltos having a last minute gossip before returning to their respective homes.

"Well, now, I don't know about everybody else," a bright, unmistakable voice sounded above the recriminations of miscounted bars and unheeded pianissimos, "but I'm off home for a lovely cup of tea—parched I am tonight . . ." and down the hill set off Mrs. Ruby Tyler to a chorus of goodnights, her cloche-hat feather bouncing jauntily into the darkness.

Now, had she said that for my benefit, I wondered as I picked up the handles of Dai's hand-truck. The offer of that damn cup of tea had been churning around in my mind for the past hour and a half—three cues I'd missed and once I'd even found myself singing with Umshla in his Recitative. Blowing hot and cold with the possibilities of the invitation I'd been and no mistake. Although, I considered, she must know how awkward it was for me—I mean, I'd even reluctantly divulged, on the understanding of the strictest confidence, the actual type of 'goods' I was picking up from Frank's van, in order to convince her of the necessity for my dead-of-night collection. Her eyes had widened in impressed surprise, I'd been gratified to notice . . . "Going really modern, aren't you?" she'd smiled with a playful tap on my arm. So she must know that I had to get my priorities right, after all—I only wished I could make up my mind what they were myself! That was all!

I had fully intended forfeiting the usual after Choir drinking session at The Prince that evening, and going straight down to the sidings to fetch my models, but, to tell the truth, my mind was in such confusion that I felt that a drink or two would help me to see things in their right perspective.

Dago Jones' old deep-bellied pram was already parked in its usual Tuesday and Saturday position in the gutter outside The Prince by the time I arrived with Dai's handtruck. Old Dago invariably managed to get blind drunk on these two nights—well—singing nights they were, you see, and if it wasn't for his wife coming to wheel him home he'd never make it past the gutter. But fair play, he wasn't all that heavy, it was just that his enormous ankle-length overcoat with its copious Poacher's pockets sewn inside, made him look a well-built man, but skin and bone he was. But Mrs. Dago Jones always had a bit of a helping hand up the hill from Dull Reggie—he couldn't resist a bit of music, so he was always hanging about outside, listening, on Tuesdays and Saturdays. They lived next door to each other anyway, in the two ramshackle cottages over the brow of the hill, their flaking lime-wash rivalling each other in their state of dilapidation. Everyone knew Dull Reggie had this thing about singing, it was just that it was a bit disconcerting when he got carried away and attempted to join in. Cy had stormed out to the vestibule of the Bethesda on more than one occasion, I can tell you, and threatened to poke him one if he didn't shut up—but you couldn't really tell him to clear off, now could you? He enjoyed it so much, if the look on his face was anything to go by—rapturous it was.

And a queer pair the Dago Joneses were too—some said they were gypsies before they settled in up at the cottage a good thirty years back, which wouldn't surprise me one bit, because Mrs. Jones was uncannily good at reading the tealeaves. It was an undisputed fact in the village—not that I'd ever consulted her myself, I left that sort of thing to the good ladies who considered it worth while tolerating the rather dubious, stale air of the dark little room in order to learn what Fate had in store for them. Although it wasn't only Fortune-telling that her reputation rested on. Many swore by her evil-smelling herb medicines as a sure cure for the Croup or the Back-Yard Trots. In fact, I know for certain, that I'd swallowed my fair share of her obnoxious mixtures when I was a lad, for Mam had been one of her most faithful customers, either dosing me up to the ears for something I had at the moment or dosing me to ward off something I might get in the future! I don't know if it had done me any good but it certainly hadn't done me any harm—although, as I eyed the empty old perambulator carriage awaiting its tenant outside The Prince, the foreboding thought suddenly occured to me as to whether the copious quantities of Mrs. Dago Jones' highly suspect herb concoctions I had reluctantly imbibed over my early developing years had somehow adversely affected my virility! I felt myself pale at the earth shattering possibility as the word 'sawdust' hammered through my brain. After all, we had been married for over five years—mind you, there was no lack of desire or anything like that—why no, I was as randy as the next man. I assured myself once more. Or was I all talk and no action? The niggling doubt depressed me even further as I stood undetermined outside The Prince. What real man, I asked myself, would have hesitated in taking up an offer of a cup of tea with Mrs. Ruby Tyler at ten o'clock at night? Damn Mrs. Dago Jones and her witch's brews, I thought viciously—it was all her fault.

"Come on, Evan," an impatient voice interrupted my self-revelations, "your pint's on the counter waiting."

With a reflective look back at the symbolically empty, scruffy old pram, I pushed open the squeaky swing doors and joined the pint-downing, cheerful crowd of choristers in the smoke-blue Bar.

P.C. Trefor Llewellyn's helmet was already in its usual place on the bottom left antler of the unfortunate deer whose glassy-eyed head was doomed to gaze down on generation after generation of Llanporth beer drinkers, while two ancient brown fly-papers blackly encrusted with the remains of the unwary, hung high on either side, a few shimmering wings and feebly struggling legs bearing witness to the still efficacy of the deadly glue. P.C. Llewellyn's presence in The Choir was of the utmost importance, there was no doubt about that—we just could not manage without him. In fact, we shuddered at the thought of his ever leaving Llanporth, not that it was likely mind, he'd been there for over twenty years and I couldn't see him handing over the lovingly tended flower garden and vegetable patch behind The Cells to any young whipper-snapper The Force might take it in their heads to send along.

You couldn't actually say that he was exactly a good tenor—nor a very profound bass for that matter. In fact, he wasn't up to much in the singing line at all, and Old Cy the Choirmaster sometimes had to ask him to sing a little quieter as he sometimes seemed to go off on a tune of his own, which unhappily bore little resemblance to anything even dreamt of by Handel or Mendelssohn. Mind you, Cy had to be very tactful about it.

"Got to get the right balance Trev, see?" he'd explain apologetically, "and that rich voice of yours drowns the tenors."

"Right you are, Cy," he'd comply with an understanding nod of the head, "it's just that I get carried away a bit with the feeling of it—you know what it's like,'' and Cy would agree that he knew exactly what it was like and we'd all keep a straight face and battle on. No, no, it wasn't his talent at singing which made him so indispensible to the choir, it was his presence in The Prince afterwards that we depended on so dearly. After all, if the only representative of The Local Constabulary was enjoying himself singing and drinking with us after hours, then there was no fear of a tap at the door and Old Mick losing his licence, now, was there? Essential he was in the choir, as I said.

Before everyone's second pint was half gone a few tentative, experimental hummings inevitably started to mingle with the smokey laughter and talk and within minutes the mournful minor of 'David of the White Rock' slowly and spontaneously swelled to fill the bar, with Umshla's clear tenor soaring to the beautiful high notes of the melody line like a bird before sinking again to the quiet, deep harmony of the last line with Frank Evans' and old Lloyd's deep bass dying away to a whisper. Real great it was—and by damn it made you thirsty!

"Thought you were going to fetch those models of yours,'' a voice sounded in my ear over the clamour of between-song discussions and re-orders. I turned to find Dai standing at my side, carefully placing a lumpy paper bag on the glass filled table.

"Where the hell have you been till now then?'' I countermanded in surprise at his sudden appearance, "We're two ahead of you, boy!''

"Well, now,'' he started to explain, "when we came out of Choir, I suddenly remembered I didn't have a scrap of bread in the house, so I thought I'd pop down to the Tugwells for some muffins to keep me going . . .''

"You crafty bugger!'' I interrupted as the light suddenly dawned, "And I suppose you walked down there with Ann Thomas and went in with her and . . . no bloody bread, indeed!''

"Well I had to have an excuse, didn't I? Fair play, and I tell you Evan,'' he went on, all serious now, "she's the one—she's definitely the one, this time. There's something about her . . .''

"Oh yeah!'' I commented sceptically, having heard similar heartfelt, rapturous declamations at least a dozen times before!

"No now, man—I mean it,'' he re-affirmed, sitting himself

down on the settle at my side and interrupting himself to thank young Alan Bevan for the pint which appeared before him. "This time is definitely it—no two ways about it." Any further discussion was prevented, however, by the outbreak of a rousing Mochyn Du (South Wales version, of course,) and within seconds Dai and I were swept into the lively chorus and singing our hearts out—for who could ever resist Mochyn Du, after all—even to discuss a new found love?

Closing Time passed without anyone bothering to notice, least of all P.C. Trefor Llewellyn, whose silvery buttoned jacket had, by now, joined his helmet on the accommodating deer's head. Large damp patches of perspiration circled darkly on his well-filled grey shirt and I knew it wouldn't be long before his collar and tie found their way up onto the dusty antlers.

"I'm taking Ann Thomas out on Saturday afternoon," Dai took the opportunity of announcing between our harmonious renditions.

"Are you, now?" I replied, suitably impressed with the speed of his conquest and jealous of his success. "Where are you going then—behind the Cricket Club?" I suggested facetiously.

"Why no, man—there's nothing like that," he replied a bit primly.

I raised a disbelieving eyebrow.

"I'm taking her to see The Bleeding Tree at Nevern—I only hope the bloody thing is still bleeding," he added, a bit worried, "it's been a bit dry lately—and she'll think I've got her on a wild goose chase if it isn't dripping." He took a thoughtful swig at his beer.

"Going in the lorry, are you?"

"No, no—on the motorbike. Ann can sit in the sidecar, see. I do hope that damn tree'll be bleeding when we get there . . ." he added as he picked up the glasses on the table and made his worried way to the crowded bar for the next round.

Song after song, major and minor, mournful and merry, continued to fill the thickening air of the bar and filter out to reach the appreciative ears of Dull Reggie who was sitting on his haunches on the pavement outside the window. The dark mahogany topped iron tables grew more damply glass-ringed, the polished spitoons rocked more dangerously, and the hand-rolled fags became more bedraggled as the evening wore on.

Henry 'Federation' was persuaded to give his yodelling an airing, and Lloyd the Stationmaster gave a solo rendering of 'Friend of Mine' while we all hummed a bit of quiet accompaniment, and by the time we'd all finished a beautiful, soul-stirring performance of 'The Missing Boat' poor old Davis the Coal was too overcome with emotion to sing any more and just sat there crying into his beer and sobbing, "A beautiful song boys—a beautiful song!" as he wiped away the tears with the back of his coal-grained hand. It was the major thirds on the last chord which really tugged at old Davis' heart-strings, he just couldn't stand it. Poignant they were after all that minor. They weren't supposed to be there, mind, but Cy loved to put them in at the end—'to lift the soul' he said—something to do with a Third of Picardie I think he said it was called. The words were damn miserable as well mind—but lovely . . .

> The child she lulls to rest—
> Lulls to rest on her breast,
> Asks, "When will father come again?"
> She dares not give reply,
> But with a heavy sigh,
> And sighing still hopes on, although all hope is vain.
> She strains her aching eyes,
> And through her tears descries,
> The phantom of a form that will come back no more.

None of your Mendelssohn and Handel in The Prince. No, no. Singing with our hearts not our brains we were, and of course, Mick's good ale helped no end. Mind you, the quality of our singing never deteriorated no matter how much liquid refreshment was imbibed, the high standard that old Cy demanded remained constant—none of your raucous rugby singing matches on a Tuesday—we left that to the Saturday night when the non-choir customers joined us with their untrained ears and larynxes. I had to admit that I enjoyed both, mind—on the appropriate night, of course.

Several times during the evening I had been on the verge of telling Dai about Mrs. Ruby Tyler's offer of a cup of tea and of my startling theory about old Mrs. Dago Jones's herbal concoctions, but I never managed to find enough time between songs, so I was still wrestling with my dilemma when Cy announced the last piece.

"Ar Hyd y Nos, boys,"

We always ended up with All Through The Night—the only song we sang completely in Welsh—not that any of us had a blind idea of what it all meant—we'd just learnt it parrot fashion off Harris the Signalman's Mam, who had lived in Llanfallteg and who could actually speak Welsh. All Through The Night just didn't sound right at all in English.

And as the last quiet harmony died away to a hush, old Mick put the towels over and called Time Gentlemen, please. I tell you, I wouldn't miss a Tuesday Choir Practice for all the tea in China. If you haven't enjoyed singing, you haven't enjoyed living,—and that's a fact.

The sight of old Dago Jones's missus standing patiently beside her pram brought back the misgivings I'd almost managed to forget in the companionship of the choir filled bar of The Prince. A rumble of thunder overhead only served to emphasise my sense of foreboding as I noticed her thin, grimy fingers clawed over the pram handle and a shudder went through me as I recalled, once more, the gallons of her obnoxious brews I had reluctantly swallowed in the past. Unbelievable concoctions mixed with those very same, witch-like hands—I thought, as I helped Frank heave old Dago into the battered old pram where he sagged in the middle like a rag doll.

"Here he is, love," announced Frank, "I see you've got a helping hand by 'ere, as usual," he added, clapping Dull Reggie on the back matily and being rewarded by the usual slow, happy smile spreading across the vacant face.

"'I must work hard', Reggie, don't forget now," I reminded with a wagging finger, but he just continued to beam round at the milling throng of well-lubricated Llanporth Choristers, before positioning himself at the rear of Prince Charming's carriage and starting to push as Mrs. Jones started pulling her load behind her up the hill. Meanwhile I was trundling off down the hill to the station with Dai's handtruck to collect my three prize beauties, but I couldn't help noticing that there was still a faint light showing through the passage window over Mrs. Ruby Tyler's front door and a thin, curling wisp of smoke rising from her chimney. Perhaps that damn kettle was still on the hob—waiting, and a shiver of excitement ran through me at the possibility, but I kept on walking, pushing the handtruck stoically before me.

Another clap of thunder rolled heavily over the Goods Sidings as I quietly pushed back the Guard's van door. I felt the dry warmth of the wood envelope me as I climbed into the gloomy darkness. Their pale, rounded feminine forms gleamed softly in the quiet shadows as they waited patiently for my arrival, the oppressive stillness of the threatened storm coupled with the effects of Mick's best ale gave a slightly uncanny feeling of unreality about the whole situation. Quickly I picked up the nearest model and clambered back out of the van, crunched across the cinder track and laid her carefully on the outspread tarpaulin on the handtruck. She stared blankly up at the starless, lowering sky, her elegant fingers reaching daintily over the sides. I gave her a re-assuring pat and returned for her companion.

Cautiously I reached out my hands to grip the dimly outlined, alabaster flanks of the second nude form, to lift her over my shoulder. It took but a split second before I realised, with mind-blinding incredulity that the sleek, rounded buttocks I was grasping so firmly were soft . . . and warm . . . and yielding! My heart thumped wildly and my brain exploded as those smooth, white arms, which only a second before had seemed so rigid, now slowly unbent and started to move towards me to wrap themselves seductively around my neck.

A vicious crack of thunder ripped open the sky above Llanporth sidings, warm cachou breath breathed into my face, soft lips brushed against my cheek, and as the faint perfume of California Poppy drifted into my reeling senses a low, unmistakable voice whispered in my unbelieving ear . . . "Hello, Mister Evan Evans—waiting for you for ages I've been!"

And as we sank to the splintered floor of old Evans' G.W.R. guardsvan, I knew that my moment of truth was at hand. This time, there was to be no escaping!

'Open the Heavens and send us relief: Help, help Thy servant now, O God! Allelujah!!!'

Chapter 4

"You might have told me you were going to lay her in the damn coffin," complained Dai as he took a spell from loading the heavy grey-stone slabs and leant gratefully against the side of Tommy Tut-Tut's boat. The air was cool and fresh after the storm of the previous night. Grey and white clouds scudded their customary eastward path across the pale blue sky—the clear-bright, false blue of the previous few days' Indian summer having faded away along with the oppressive, cloying heat.

"A bloody start it gave me, I can tell you, when I went in this morning, seeing her lying there staring up at me all white and pale."

"Well I didn't prop her up because that one isn't too steady on her feet and I didn't want to risk her toppling over and breaking an arm or anything." I explained, giving my fag paper an expert lick and a quick rolling seal. Mind you, I'd been in a bit of a hurry the previous night, what with one thing and the other it had been almost midnight by the time I'd eventually carried spare Tabitha into Dai's Coffin Shed, as previously arranged, before making my hasty way home with her other two companions. Just made it before the rain started to pelt down too.

I hadn't been able to find Tabitha at first—Mrs. Ruby Tyler had tucked her away, flat on the floor on the far side of the van, with her own clothes piled neatly on top—and a good job too, because if I'd climbed into that van and seen four nudes standing there staring at me I'd have bolted there and then! Which would have been a pity really—although I wouldn't have this damn splinter in my knee if I had!

"What on earth are you doing with that needle, Evan?" Myra had asked in surprise when she'd come into the bedroom with my early cup of tea that morning and caught me poking away at the irritating thorn in my flesh.

"Oh, it's nothing, love," I explained guiltily, "just a bit of a splinter from Dai's old ladder—must have got it when I was up at the school yesterday. His overalls are a bit on the thin side . . . I think I'll leave it and let it work its way out," I added, replacing the needle in the pincushion on the dressing table, and taking the proferred cup of tea gratefully.

"I'll be helping Dai out with shifting some stones for Captain Rees-Williams' new boundary wall this afternoon," I announced with a tactical change of subject, "All right for you to look after the shop, is it?"

She nodded in easy agreement as we'd sat on the edge of the bed for a few minutes enjoying the refreshing first drink of the day.

"What time did you get home last night, then?" Myra had asked reflectively as she sipped at the steaming cup. "I waited up till gone eleven, but I didn't like that old thunder so I pulled all the curtains, covered up the mirrors and went to bed . . . go to The Prince for your sing-song before you went down to the railway after all, did you?"

"Yes . . . yes, that was it." I'd hastily agreed, "I didn't like to miss it really—and it went on a bit late, as usual . . . you know . . ." I finished lamely.

"You and your sing-song . . ." she smiled.

"Come and see what I brought home from Cardiff, then," I'd announced, placing our empty cups on the chest of drawers. "Something special, it is," I'd declared grandly as I took hold of her arm with one hand, clutched my cordless pyjama trousers with the other and led us ceremoniously down the narrow stairs. Somewhat mystified, Myra had followed me to the back room behind the shop.

"There!" I'd proclaimed with a flourish as I'd thrown the door open to reveal my two lovely models. "What do you think of that?"

Myra gave a gasp of admiration and surprise and then, to my amazement, burst out laughing— really dissolved into uncontrollable shrieks, she did, holding her sides and pointing at my lovely models, then at me and back at the silent, reproachful nudes as renewed waves of laughter swept over her until the tears were running down her cheeks. I just couldn't understand it.

"What's so funny, then?" I'd asked, a little put out by her unexpected reaction. I stared at the models, but they were just the same—nothing particularly hilarious that I could see.

"Oh . . . Evan . . . !" she'd eventually managed to gasp, wiping her wet eyes, "When I went down to the pump for a can of water for tea this morning, Mrs. Know-all Jones was there . . ." more chuckles bubbled to the surface before she could continue . . . "and do you know what she told me and Mrs.Frank Evans?" I shook my head in complete bewilderment.

"She said, that last night, the thunder had woken her up and when she was looking out of the bedroom window she saw . . . a man carrying a naked woman across the railway sidings and disappear behind the wall!" I gulped nervously as another wave of laughter swept over Myra.

"It was you, wasn't it?" she laughed, "You and one of those?" she pointed a shaking finger at the disdainful creature.

I managed a sickly grin. "Yes . . . yes . . . it must have been, I suppose," I agreed, succeeding in raising a few forced ha ha's to accompany my confession. Bloody hell, I'd thought, just shows how careful you had to be. All I could hope was that the old battle-axe hadn't seen anything else.

"Isn't it a scream, Evan?" Myra had chuckled, "Just wait till I tell everybody! Fancy Mrs. Know-All Jones believing there was a man down in the sidings with a real naked woman!"

Fancy! I thought, as the sweat trickled down my back.

I hadn't intended to put my models in the window until Friday, so that Myra and I could spend half-day closing on Thursday dressing them up to perfection, but it suddenly flashed through my mind that if I told Myra to keep the models a secret until then, the whole village would be rife with suspicion and conjecture as to who the 'naked' lady might be! And you never knew what might turn up as everyone speculatively eyed everyone else. What if somebody happened to remember that Mr. Tyler was away that night? What if somebody saw Mrs. Ruby Tyler going out 'for a walk' after Choir? There was only one thing for it—I had to get those damn models in the window that very day—for after all I still wanted the satisfaction of beholding the impact their unanticipated appearance would have on every League of the feminine populace of Llanporth. Otherwise, my long and closely guarded secret would all have been in vain. At least, now they would all be so busy laughing and joking about the misunderstanding down at the Railway Sidings that it wouldn't give them the opportunity to speculate on anything more scandalous!

Never again! I vowed—Never again—as I hurriedly climbed back upstairs with my trailing pyjamas. Oh, what tangled webs we weave, I thought as I winced as that damn splinter pricked my knee at every step . . . bloody rabbit boxes!

There had been no time for any breakfast. Myra had excitedly ransacked the shop shelves, feverishly examining and discarding frocks, skirts, blouses and cardigans in an attempt to find the most stunning outfits to clothe the models. Alice and Maud, she'd named them, after a thoughtful minute spent studying their rosebud-pouting expressions. Like a child with a new toy she'd been, frantically struggling with uncooperative stiff arms as she'd tried to cloth Alice in the fetching, hastily flat-ironed, pale green frock which she had finally chosen, leaving me to search the top shelf for one of the latest jazz patterned cardigans to go with it.

"I just can't get it on her!" she'd gasped as she stood in the shop back doorway, her face flushed with agitation, her hair disarrayed from the abortive struggle to clothe stubborn Alice. "I can get one arm in, but not the other!" she'd declared somewhat wildly, casting a fretful eye on the clock, "Oh, and look, Evan, only another half an hour we've got before we open."

"I'll come and give you a hand—there's a knack to it I expect," I suggested soothingly as I climbed down from the step ladder with the necessary jazz cardigan.

"I've tried it over her head, but that was no use, so I put it on her feet first—but look—it's got stuck half way!" she lamented as we stood viewing the crazily half-clothed Alice.

"Leave it to me, girl," I advised confidently.

Five minutes later, however, we were no nearer attiring Alice or Maud, in spite of having tried various methods of procedure, all of which had been effectively thwarted by the rigidly disdainful creatures.

"There must be a way," I grunted as I wrestled energetically with the unco-operative Alice.

"Mind, or you'll rip it!" Myra shrieked as an ominous sound of tearing stitches rent the air.

"Aw hell," I gasped, defeated. "I'm sure Cardiff Hughes never had all this trouble."

Suddenly I had a flash of insight. Cardiff Hughes often had models standing about with no arms on at all! That was it of course! The stupid old arms came off!

At last, with nine minutes left to spare, we'd both stood back with a sigh of relief and viewed the now satisfactorily attired models—Alice in her pale green frock and zig-zag jazz cardigan with a pair of white kid gloves elegantly balanced across the palm of one outstretched hand and a shiny patent leather handbag dangling from the other. And Maud in a fashionable navy blue worsted coat over the latest pouched blouse and skirt with a matching cloche hat with a peacock-blue feather and an imitation silk scarf casually draped over her arm.

"Oh Evan," Myra had breathed, lost in admiration at our handiwork. "They're lovely, really lovely!" and I'd nodded in agreement, well satisfied with the results of my enterprise.

"Oh!" she'd suddenly gasped, clasping her hand over her mouth in horror and turning to me with her eyes wide and staring. "Evan," she'd whispered in dismay," they haven't got any knickers on!"

"Well, that doesn't matter, girl," I'd laughed, "nobody's going to know, are they, after all?"

"But we can't put them in the window without any on . . . we just can't. What if they fell over or something . . ." she ended up lamely.

My laughter increased to a roar at the prospect.

"No, Evan, I mean it now. Go and get two pairs of the salmon pink directoire. Go on."

Well, there was no point in arguing about it, not when she felt so strongly, after all. "Short or longlegs?" I shouted back from the shop.

"Better make it short—in case they show."

Returning into the kitchen with the necessary garments of modesty, I threw one pair over to Myra, tilted Maud unceremoniously over against the grandfather clock and started to fit her rigid little feet into the legs of the salmon pink directoire, with a deliberately lascivious chuckle.

"I'll do them both, thank you very much, Evan," came the rather pointed remark at my elbow and there stood Myra with one of her old-fashioned looks in her eye.

"I was only joking, girl," I pointed out with a grin. "Anyway, there's not much fun in putting the damn things *on* now is there, fair play?"

She tutted a reproof but failed to suppress a smile as she ordered me to go and clear a space in the window. "Only three minutes we've got before the blinds go up, mind,'' she reminded, as she bent to her task.

There followed a few hectic, hair-raising minutes as Alice and Maud were steered carefully through the narrow passageway and manoeuvred painstakingly into the waiting window, but as the clock struck nine I backed breathlessly out, leaving the elegant pair awaiting their debut behind the still lowered blind.

There's a morning we had! The impact of the revelation of my closely guarded secret proving more successful than my wildest dreams. Myra and I had gleefully watched the astonished double-takes as the local ladies had given the window their usual casual glance in passing, only to stop dead in their tracks and stare in amazement at the unexpected sight.

Mrs. Nellie Williams had been the first past the window, on her way back from Shorty Howes the Bread. In she'd come, pinging the door open excitedly, full of 'Well I never!' and 'Fancy now!' as she marvelled at our enterprise, her warm loaves filling the air with their yeast freshness causing rumbling pangs of hunger in my empty stomach from my missed breakfast.

That pretty little Rosie George from the Valleys was next to stand and stare, soon to be joined by Mrs. Know-All Jones, whose startled expression was worth every penny Cardiff Hughes was going to get out of me. I could tell she was tamping mad that she hadn't heard a whisper of Alice and Maud's presence in advance and down on the pavement with a heavy bang went her two cans of water and back down the hill she rushed to get in first with spreading the news at her favourite gossiping post down at the pump.

Little Bertha Gwillam carefully wedged her enormous perambulator against the wall, never having trusted the brake since it had gone careering headlong down the hill on its own a month back, its perilous trip brought to a timely halt only by the chance presence of Young Umshla out on one of his vegetable deliveries. In she came, all bright eyed, her dark curls still tangled from bed, to ask the price of the green dress on the lady in the window, her face falling a little as Myra told her 22/11d.

"I'll have to ask my Stan,'' she murmured reluctantly as she made her way out, standing to stare longingly at Alice for another good five minutes before continuing her hazardous way down the hill, pulling back on her heels to prevent her noble baby carriage running away with her.

We didn't actually sell very much that first morning, mind—but, by damn we had a record number of customers in! Packed out we were at times, more like a Women's Institute than a Draper's—everyone chattering, admiring and laughing as Myra told and re-told the saga of Mrs. Know-All Jones seeing a man with a naked woman down at the Railway Sidings, and all the time it was her Evan with his models! I tell you, I've never grinned so many sickly grins in my life as I did that morning, and everytime that damn door pinged open my empty stomach lurched uncontrollably in case it was Mrs. Ruby Tyler. Well, it's different, isn't it, after all, in the cold light of the next morning? Fair play.

And Mrs. Know-All Jones, finding the centre of interest and gossip having moved from the water pump up to Evans the Drapers, promptly pushed her way in and sat herself down on our best bent-wood customers' chair and there she stayed for the entire morning, greeting each new customer as they came in and regaling them with the Railway Sidings Saga while her forgotten water cans stood on the pavement outside, their contents explored by the investigating dirty fingers of Dull Reggie. Needless to say, he didn't manage to get to school at all that morning! Absolutely enchanted he was by Alice and Maud, his eyes rarely leaving them for a second as he constantly scanned them from head to toe, mouthing who knows what greetings to them through the dividing glass, his slow-witted mind capturing and savouring, with pleasurable bewilderment, some of the excitement of the almost festive air of commotion created by the comings and goings of our gossiping, laughing customers. Well, a good excuse it was for them, after all, to have a break from the dull housework routine of the usual Wednesday morning in Llanporth.

"Ay, it was well worth keeping them a secret, Dai," I confided as we squeezed a final puff from our fagends before starting once more on loading Tommy Tut-Tut's boat with the heavy stones from the old disused jetty. I'd left Myra happily coping with the shop for the afternoon, but I must admit, I'd been glad to get changed into my old clothes and get out into the fresh air to help Dai. I mean, I liked success as much as the next man, but by damn, those women could talk! And I'd just about had enough of Mrs. Know-All Jones leerily winking at me everytime the Railway Sidings were mentioned—unnerving it was, man, I mean—if she only knew . . . it had almost put me off my dinner thinking about it.

"No point in breaking our backs carting these damn stones up to the lorry," Dai had pointed out when I'd first arrived and found him putting the stones into the bottom of the beached boat.

"We'll just load them by 'ere, nice and handy, wait till the tide comes in and then she'll float off and I'll take her down the harbour to the Captain's place—right on the shore his land is—couldn't be easier. Three or four trips should do it, I reckon."

"What time's High Tide then?" I asked as we placed the final stone of the load in the boat.

"About five to half-past. A good Spring Tide it is—it'll float her off lovely. Fancy giving me a hand for a couple of hours shifting my chicken houses onto that new land of mine, Evan? And you can tell me what you intend doing with that bloody model whose stuck in my coffin while you're about it, too."

As we strolled up to Dai's yard I gave him a brief outline of my plan for making damaged Tabitha earn her keep.

"Bloody good idea that, Evan," he agreed as we turned into the gateway. "I'll sound 'em out tonight—two bob, you said, for the evening?"

"That's it, boy—it'll only work out at about a penny each, see, so I should think that's about the right price. You may as well take her down with you on the handcart—wrap her up well mind, we don't want the women finding out about her—you know what some of 'em are like . . . sure to complain, they would."

"Aye, you're damn right there, boy," he agreed with a grin, "Old Frank's wife would stop him going for a start! and Umshla's Mam . . . dominated they are boy, half of 'em." he ended with a sad shake of his head at the lack of backbone in the male community of Llanporth.

"Does Myra know then?" he asked.

"Well . . . no . . . I didn't think it was worth bothering her with having to keep the secret from the others see?"

"Aye," he agreed, "better if no women know at all really."

71

All except Mrs. Ruby Tyler, I thought to myself apprehensively. I had been very tempted to tell Dai all about my stupendous activities of the previous night—it would have been great to see the look of incredulity on his face. Mind, I'd often boasted to him of the various conquests I'd made over the years—ever since we were lads, and he'd never doubted for a second that what I'd told him was gospel. But made up they were—every damn one. But, after all, I had to pretend to keep up with him didn't I! It was all part of the relationship we had. And now when I had a real one to boast about at last, I couldn't bring myself to risk it! A devil it was. But the way he walked the tight wire and pushed his luck with his own fate, like when he'd asked Old Rees to check the damn measurements—well, I just couldn't chance his making a slip-up with my secret! Pity that.

We managed to shift most of the chicken houses and runs by half past four and we were just having a bit of a sit down and a cup of tea in the coffin shed when Dai drew thoughtfully on his Woodbine and announced out of the blue,

"I nipped over to 'The Farmer's' at Llanston Cross at dinnertime—on the old motorbike."

I raised an eyebrow.

"Sid Phelps told me Sybil wanted to see me." he added, taking another deep draw down to his socks.

Sybil was the well renowned barmaid at The Farmer's. Although I had to admit that I had never actually seen the young lady myself, preferring to confine my drinking to The Prince, everyone knew she was very generous with her favours —especially after hours in the old dairy behind the pub.

"She's in the club." he stated flatly.

"Never!" I exclaimed, "Bloody hellfire!"
I laughed, "Who's the lucky father then?"

"She says it's my bloody fault!"
I felt the smile stiffen on my face.

"It isn't mind!" he hastily added, seeing my look of horror. "I tell you boy, I haven't been there since last May—that's nearly five months."

"Does she look at all . . .?" I rounded my hands expressively in front of my stomach.

"Why no. Flat as a bloody pancake she is."

"You told her straight then, that she'd made a mistake?"

"Why aye, course I did—but she wouldn't have it. Insists it was my fault. Says she's got dates and all to prove it."

"Bugger the dates—it's a different one each night by what I've heard—I mean, everybody's been there haven't they, after all?" I reasoned.

"Aye . . . all except bloody you!" he pointed out, half joking.

There it is again, I thought despondently as the nagging doubt about the extent of my virility rose once more into my mind. I had lain awake most of the night trying to take a new analysing look at myself. I had forced myself to admit that if it had been left to me I'd never have knocked on Mrs. Ruby Tyler's door for that proferred cup of tea.

All talk I was. I had to be honest with myself. I mean, what if Ann Thomas had invited me into the store cupboard up at the school, when all the kids had gone home? I'd have found some excuse in spite of all the thoughts I'd had about her when I was safely up the top of the ladder. That damned medicine it was, I was sure, and I cursed Mrs. Dago Jones and her herbs. None of my friends had swallowed half as much of the stuff as I had—and Dai had never been forced to touch a drop—he was always so damned healthy. I'd have to do something about it, for my own peace of mind.

"I've never even met the girl—or been to The Farmer's, man, fair play." I retorted, excusing my lack of experience in the old dairy behind the pub. "Anyway," I went on, reverting to the original topic under discussion, "I wonder why she picked on you? I mean, there have been plenty of others all through the summer."

"Blowed if I know," he replied, his normally happy face clouded with concern.

"She must think you're a good catch—with the business and all . . ."

"She told me I'd have to marry her."

"Never!"

"Well, she's damn well not going to have me and that's that. Only a bit of fun it was man, nothing serious. I'll swear this is none of my doing." Dai paused. "I told her mind."

"You managed to talk her out of it, then?" I asked with some relief.

"Well, not exactly, but I think she'll try and choose

73

somebody else a bit more easy going and who can't remember dates!'' There was a pause. ''I hope.'' he added with a worried frown.

''Keep away from the place, Dai,'' I advised.

''Don't you worry boy, that's just what I'm going to do . . . and come on,'' he said, looking at his watch, ''it's nearly half past five. That damn boat'll be floating out on its own if we don't get down there.''

Poor old Dai, I thought as we made our way down the hill. He certainly has plenty on his mind—and there's me worrying because I've got a splinter in my knee!

The light, freshening breeze met us as we rounded the corner to the harbour. The shingle beach of a few hours ago had disappeared under the flecked expanse of the incoming tide and we cast our eyes across to the spot in the distance where we'd loaded Tommy Tut-Tut's boat. But there was nothing. Just the green water lapping up against the old wall.

''Be damned if we're not too late—she's floated off on her own,'' exclaimed Dai in annoyance as he scanned the estuary for the missing boat.

''It can't have drifted far,'' I pointed out as we hurried along the crumbling stone jetty to the place where we'd removed the stones. We peered over the side.

''Well, I'll be . . .'' breathed Dai in disbelief.

There, rippling beneath the waves was the dim outline of poor old Tommy Tut-Tut's boat, sitting on the bottom, firmly anchored down by the stones we had so carefully placed in her!

''It's just not my bloody day today,'' he grumbled sourly, ''I'll be glad when it's bloody tomorrow!'' and he turned on his heel and left me staring at the swirling green water which slapped mockingly against the old stone jetty at my feet, as a hysterical laugh rose in my throat.

*   *   *

''Mrs. L. Y. T. Jones told me she saw Mrs. Ruby Tyler down at the Doctor's surgery this evening,'' Myra announced with a smile as she carefully replaced the cosy over the teapot.

I halted in mid chew.

''Oh yes,'' I managed to reply.

''Well, you can imagine what she thought she was there for

can't you? I mean, there's nothing wrong with her, is there? She was at Choir last night anyway, wasn't she?''

''Er . . . yes . . . I think she was there . . .'' I replied, noisily swallowing a lump of cheese which seemed to have got stuck in my throat through a sudden lack of saliva.

''Mrs. L. Y. T. Jones had the months all counted out to next April,'' she laughed, and my appetite for supper suddenly vanished. Good God, I thought, she can't know that quick, as I frantically counted up my own nine months and arrived at June! I seemed to be dogged by that ominous nine month time lapse today, I thought as Dai's predicament flashed through my mind.

''And then,'' Myra went on, ''Mrs. Know-All Jones came over to us at the Women's Institute tonight and told us what Mrs. Ruby Tyler had really gone there for.''

''Oh yes,'' I repeated, my talent for conversation appearing to have become rather stilted, as I made a great show of taking an enormous sip of tea which almost choked me.

''Well now,'' and Myra gave a deep chuckle, ''it seems that her damn old cat had been sunning itself on the side of the lav seat and had sharpened its claws on the rim. Two great long splinters in her behind Ruby got!'' I gave a weak laugh which was drowned by Myra's chortles of amusement.

''There's embarrassing it must have been for her to go and ask that young doctor to get them out for her,'' she chattered on, as my mind filled with the picture of Frank Evans' Guards van with its splintered rabbit boxes and equally splintered floor.

''Now, I'd have asked you to get them out for me, wouldn't I, Evan?'' I nodded. ''But I don't think Mr. and Mrs. Tyler are like that. I think she's a bit shy underneath, don't you?''

My mental picture of rabbit boxes changed to a fleeting recollection of Mrs. Ruby Tyler's soft, milk-white thighs and biting pearly teeth. I blinked quickly, ''Yes, I think she is a bit shy . . .'' I agreed, fumbling frantically in my pocket for a packet of Rizzla papers and my tin of tobacco. Well, I had to have something to do with my hands . . . and a bloody awful fag I made too—the worst in my life.

For the second night running, I hardly slept a wink and when I did there was the barmaid of The Farmer's showing everybody her splinters—all over her they were—and accusing me of putting her in the club, while I stood in the middle of a sinking boat, surrounded by a silent ring of Llanporth Choir members and naked models, valiantly trying to keep the tenor line of "Ar Hyd Y Nos" going all on my own, with the dread certainty that if I stopped singing the whole world would come crashing down about me.

Never again, I vowed in my sleep, as my hand scratched at the irritating sliver of incriminating timber in my knee. Never again.

Chapter 5

I awoke the following morning with my mind firmly made up. I was going to tackle old Dago Jones's Missus about her damned medicines that very day. The only problem was to think of a plausible enough excuse for visiting her in their notoriously mucky little cottage. If anyone saw me going in or coming out, heaven knows what interpretation might be put on it. After all, nobody called on Mrs. Dago Jones openly these days, her clientel having considerably deteriorated since mam used to buy her curative and preventative medicines there twenty odd years before. Preventative being the operative word, it would now appear, I thought gloomily as I considered the possibility of her ever having put bromide in any of the concoctions she'd brewed up for me. I mean the effect might have been both cumulative and delayed, you never could tell. No-one would deny, mind, that she still had her share of unseen visitors—stealthily tapping at the back door after dark for potions for this, charms for that, slippery elm for a 'friend' and various other darkly private requests. No, I just couldn't risk being spotted, not with my position in the community.

I sat up in bed and thoughtfully rolled my first fag of the day, the aromatic smell of newly lit paraffin and the clank of the kettle on the stove downstairs reminded me that I had another good five minutes to give to the problem before Myra returned with the cups of tea.

I inhaled deeply and concentrated my thoughts. The solution came to me in a flash. It was so simple that I chuckled aloud to myself with relief—I would openly go and call on Mrs. Dago Jones purely as an act of charity—and Dull Reggie's Mam and her ill-clothed brood lived next door so I could call on them too, just as an extra red herring doubly to ensure my good character.

I could take my old grey worsted jacket, that thickened green pullover with the darned elbows, my . . . I jumped out of bed and hastily searched through the chest of drawers, turning out shrunken vests, old shirts, matted socks and anything else I could possibly discard in order to put the first stage of my plan into operation. Impatiently I flung open the doors of the huge mahogany wardrobe and eyed its dark contents with a critical eye, my gaze coming to rest on Pa's old flannel suit he used to swelter in each summer.

I'll never wear it, I thought, but my hand hesitated on the hanger. It didn't seem right, somehow, giving Pa's suit away to dirty old Dago Jones. But after all, I reasoned with myself, it was for a good cause—the future continuation of the Evans family name might depend on it. And with that worthy thought in mind I lifted it out and laid it on the bed alongside the rest of my unwanted clothes.

"Myra!" I shouted down the stairs, "Have you got any old clothes you want to get rid of?"

My plan was underway.

*   *   *

Sales in the shop rocketed that morning, with Alice and Maud each now resplendent in a different outfit which Myra had chosen the previous night. The good ladies of Llanporth, with each League well represented, pinged open the door as they had done the day before, but this time with the necessary money in their purses, no doubt wheedled out of their reluctant husbands by various ways the night before. It wasn't long before it became apparent that to acquire and wear a 'Model' garment was going to become a point of one-up-manship amongst the female community. I think we'd even have sold extra pairs of salmon pink directoire knickers if they had known that Alice and Maud were sporting them! But unfortunately those nether garments remained unseen. Pity really.

Pa's old tailoring room at the back of the shop was in constant use that morning with customers trying on dresses and blouses, skirts and coats, with Myra surreptitiously substituting larger sizes where necessary while giving earnest assurance that it was the exact one which had just come off the model!

Meanwhile I spent almost the entire morning clambering in and out of the shop window, much to Dull Reggie's delight, clutching first Alice and then Maud, retreating to the back kitchen, stripping their clothes off, handing them to Myra's impatiently outstretched hand, dressing them up again, struggling back through the passage and each time pushing past Mrs. Know-All Jones who was once more ensconced on our best customers' chair telling everyone her latest bit of news about Selina Rees-Williams meeting a very swanky young man off the train that very morning.

I had just staggered back to the window with Maud for the fourth time when the door pinged open heralding yet another customer to join the three already in the shop. An unmistakable cloud of Californian Poppy drifted towards my twitching nostrils, my knees turned to water, my hands went clammy and I felt the colour drain from my face as I made a great show of re-arranging the button cards on the floor of the shop window, delaying that inevitable moment when I would have to turn round and face . . . could I call her my mistress? After only once? Or did that imply a regular carrying on? My mind buzzed with the tortuous definition as the raucous voice of Mrs. Know-All Jones filled my ears.

"No good offering you my chair, is it Mrs. Tyler?" followed by great guffaws of knowing laughter exploding from the voluminous depths of her Double O.X. chest. "Nasty old things, splinters," she went on, giving a mental dig in the ribs to everybody in the shop.

Shut up you old cow, I thought viciously, and get your fat behind off my best customers' chair.

"No thank you Mrs. Jones," came the acid polite reply, "I always maintain that too much sitting about makes your hips spread . . . Good morning Mrs. Evans, Good morning Mr. Evans," came the dreaded greeting.

I turned, a well simulated look of surprise on my face. "Oh, good morning, Mrs. Tyler . . . I didn't see you come in . . ."

"Perhaps you need glasses then, Mr. Evans," she joked, "You'll have to get Mrs. Evans there to feed you up with carrots. You'll be able to see in the dark then, as well!" And she gave a split second, but unmistakable direct look into my eyes.

Aw gawd! I thought as the dim interior of Frank's model-filled guard's van flashed before my eyes, why do I have to go and get myself mixed up with people who push their luck. Her and Dai! What a pair!

"Yes, indeed," I managed to laugh back.

"Quite a commotion you're making here in Llanporth with your models," she went on, "Everybody's talking about them.

What with the lovely clothes they're wearing in your window by there and that mix-up at the Railway sidings!"

I joined in weakly with the general chuckles.

"Do you know," she went on, smiling that crimson smile at everyone, "I hardly slept a wink that night, what with the thunder and one thing and the other!" There was a chorus of 'neither did I' from the ladies, as my stomach tied itself in knots. Good God! It sounded as if half of Llanporth were awake and listening that damn night, I thought with growing dismay. And I vowed for the umpteenth time, never again! Never again! While a nagging little demon, born of my distrust of Mrs. Dago Jones's medicines whispered 'Coward!' in the back of my distracted mind.

"Evan! . . . Evan!" Myra's repeated calling brought me back to my surroundings with a jolt. "Would you take Model Number Two," (she didn't like the customers to know they had names) "into the kitchen and take off the brown silk frock for Mrs. Tyler to try on please?"

Damn me, I thought, feeling drained of all mental and physical energy, I only put the bloody thing on her five minutes ago! Thank heavens it was half-day closing!

Think of the profit, man, think of the profit, I repeated with deliberately induced calm, as I clambered back into the window to confront the gormlessly beaming face of Dull Reggie once more.

At least he was enjoying himself, I thought, as I watched him slowly extract an unwrapped doorstep of a jam sandwich from his coat pocket. The Llanporth Council School was to be deprived of his presence for yet another day it seemed!

Poor bugger, I thought sympathetically, he doesn't realise it's early closing today. I hope he doesn't wait all the afternoon for the blinds to go up after dinner.

*   *   *

It was gone five before I eventually managed to set out, well Dressed for Drapery still, for Mrs. Dago Jones's cottage, my prominently displayed charity clothes tucked under each arm. Myra had been a bit surprised at my sudden generosity of spirit, but I'd explained that I'd seen the Dago Joneses and Dull Reggie outside The Prince after Choir and I'd noticed what a deplorable state their clothes had been in—not to mention Reggie's sister's lack of a decent frock when I'd noticed her on her way to scrub out after school. Myra's clothes would just about fit her a treat.

Myra had wanted to wrap all the clothes up neatly in a brown paper parcel, but I'd managed to talk her out of it. "I'll just roll them up under my arm," I'd suggested casually. Well, after all, I wanted as many people as possible to see what I was taking up to the Joneses, otherwise the whole point of my cleverly thought out subterfuge would be lost. I'd tried to get out earlier but there'd been so much book-keeping and special re-ordering from Cardiff Hughes to do after our record sales. And Myra had been late getting the dinner because we had been so busy in the shop.

"How much did the models cost, Evan?" she'd asked as she'd noticed me writing out the cheque.

"Seven pounds," I'd answered without thinking.

"That's three pounds ten each."

"Er . . . yes . . . that's right . . ." I'd agreed, having forgotten for the moment that she knew nothing of Tabitha. "But it's a good investment," I'd added hastily as I noticed her face cloud over slightly at the seeming extravagance.

"Of course . . . you're right," she smiled, "Look at this morning!"

"Mind you," I'd warned, "We can't expect to keep that pace up, but I'm sure they'll earn their keep."

"Things have certainly changed since they arrived anyway, haven't they?"

"Yes," I nodded, feelingly, "but I'll soon . . . we'll soon," I hastily corrected myself, "get back to normal!" And that little horned demon in the back of my head had chuckled to himself as I'd picked up my bundles of clothing and made my way through the blind-darkened, disarrayed shop and out onto the pavement.

The subdued High Street had its usual sterile air of Thursday Early-closing as I made my conspicuous way up the hill. Deserted it was, except for Dilys Davies's youngest who was sitting on the kerb edge, painstakingly chalking a pattern on his top, ready for giving it a good whipping down the hill. A lovely surface for tops the High Street had, I remembered. Nice and smooth, even if there was a bit of a stiff camber down to the gutters on either side. The art was to keep the spinning top right on the crest in the middle of the road, and with a bit of luck and skill you'd be able to make it right down to the station.

"Nice top you've got there, Selwyn," I remarked in passing.

"It's me Pa's." he stated briefly, without looking up from his engrossing task, as if that were enough pedigree for any self-respecting top.

I wonder where my old whip and top are, I pondered as I continued the climb. I was sure I'd never given them away. I'd have a look in the attic when I got home. Perhaps one day my son would proudly be able to say 'It's me Pa's', and the thought brought me back with a jerk to the prime motive for my journey up the hill that quiet afternoon and I set my mind to devising a suitable opening sentence to introduce the rather delicate reason for my visit to Mrs. Dago Jones.

The strains of repeatedly erratic semiquaver runs with the inevitable missing F sharps, reached my ears as I neared the Baptist Schoolroom. Miss Davies is hammering her lonely way through her usual piano practice, I thought, wincing as a jangle of notes tripped over each other to their customary discordant climax. Poor dab, I thought, sitting in that big old room all on her own, practising her heart out. And no thanks she'll get for it—only more complaints next Tuesday because she can't keep up with the choir.

I poked my head round the door.

"It's coming on lovely!" I called, my voice echoing hollowly in the high empty vaults above. Well, it was worth lying, wasn't it, just to see the look of surprised delight on her face—really lit up it did. She even looked quite pleasant without her customary harrassed expression. I'd always thought of her as old, but come to think of it she couldn't be much over thirty-five.

Perhaps I'd have a quiet word with old Cy next Tuesday and suggest we take the Zardoc a shade slower, just to give her a chance, I considered as I continued on my way, leaving Miss Gwendoline Davies attacking her semiquavers with renewed enthusiasm behind me.

I gave the bundle of clothes under my arm a deliberately conspicuous hitch-up as I drew near the Top Pump where Alf the Lion's missus was standing astride the puddle drawing her can of water and Mrs. L. Y. T. Jones stood patiently awaiting her turn.

"'Afternoon Mr. Evans," she greeted, eyeing my bundle curiously. "Out for a bit of a stroll?" she hinted.

"Well, not really," I replied and went on to tell her, with great satisfaction, of my intended charitable visits to Dull Reggie's Mam and to Mrs. Dago Jones, for although the High Street had been deserted, I knew, with the certainty which only a native of Llanporth could have, that at least a dozen pairs of unseen, curious eyes had plotted my progress up the hill with my bundle of clothes, from the veiled safety of their heavily net-curtained windows.

'Where's Evans the Draper off to then?' I could imagine them wondering, and who better, (apart from Mrs. Know-All Jones) to impart the necessary information, than Mrs. L. Y. T. Jones?

As the houses thinned out the air thickened with the pungent, ripe scent of overhanging purple elderberry and the hedges grew warmly crimson with the hue of hip and haw. It was going to be a hard winter, I thought, eyeing the profusion of glowing berries, and I made a mental note to put an extra order in for woollen underwear and fleecy lined liberty bodices from Cardiff Hughes. There was nothing like a bit of sharp frost for sending the Llanporth population scampering after a bit of cosy comfort, no matter what League they were in!

I was still no nearer finding a suitable way to broach the subject of my problem with Mrs. Dago Jones when I eventually arrived at the pair of ramshackle, dirty lime-washed cottages on the crest of the hill. There was no sign of Mrs. Williams's brood of children as I made my way across the small patch of trampled sparse grass strewn with empty cockle shells, purporting to be the front garden. Gingerly I stepped over a few rusty pieces of tin, a sad-faced, armless doll and an upturned bucket with a hole in the bottom before navigating my way past a scrawny rooster with a wicked eye perched on a mildew rollered mangle only to find the doorway blocked by an evil smelling pram, whose contents, in the shape of a hollow-bellied cat, lay purring on a stained grey blanket, contentedly suckling her three blind, ravenous kittens.

I edged my way past and knocked. The purring rose to a gentle crescendo as the cat became aware of my presence and a murmur of voices reached me from inside. The latch clicked, the door opened a fraction and a small sticky face peered out at the level of my knee.

I cleared my throat. "Is your Mam in?" But the dirty little face just continued to stare up at me.

"Go and tell your Mam." I encouraged, but the gaze remained blank. By damn, I thought, there was another Dull Reggie here by the look of it. I was just about to give another tap when the door suddenly opened wide to reveal the pinafore-bursting figure of Mrs. Williams, a bare-bummed infant perched on her eight-month-gone bump.

Hastily I explained my reason for calling, holding out the bundle of clothes as proof of my good intentions.

"Come in, come in, Mr. Evans," she welcomed with a fat smile, pushing the little one out of the doorway and stepping back for me to ease my way past her temporarily increased girth.

I murmured my thanks as I ducked my head under the lintel and entered the dark little room. The foetid air of unwashed bodies and the sickly sharp smell of stale baby's vomit hit me like a physical blow, making me gasp with dismay. A circle of faces gazed wonderingly at me from around a littered table and I looked in vain for somewhere to put my charity clothes in the cramped dark little room.

"Here you are Mr. Evans," Mrs. Williams directed, shooing another cat off a chair and begging me to sit down.

"Hello then," I smiled round at the sea of jammy faces as I gingerly perched myself on the edge of the proferred seat. Good God, I thought, where on earth do they all sleep? For there were only two rooms in the cottage I knew for a fact. Perhaps they turned the table upside-down!

Dull Reggie beamed vacantly at my greeting and a slow rivulet of tea trickled down his chin as his mouth hung open awaiting the next bit of bread and jam which was poised, forgotten, in mid-air.

"Now then, you must have a nice cup of tea Mr. Evans," pressed Mrs. Williams, picking up a mug from the table and throwing the dregs onto the fire with an accuracy of aim which could only have come from long practice, before ordering her Lily to go and give it a swill from the can outside.

"No, no, it's quite all right," I interrupted hastily as Lily started to get up from the table, "Mrs. Evans is just making my tea at home, so I can't stop—and I've got to call in next door with this suit for Dago and a few things for Mrs. Jones. Having a bit of a clear out at home we were, you see," I explained as I carefully edged my way past another miniature female version of Dull Reggie who was aimlessly poking her blacknailed fingers down the row of spar holes of her backless chair. Her dark, nit-flecked hair hung in tangled, matted hanks over her eyes and I remembered the horror Mam had felt when she'd discovered some nits in my own hair just after I'd started school in The Babies' Class. Raked my head with a fine tooth comb we had, night after night, while I'd watched, fascinated but unashamed, as the crawly little creatures and their white eggs had fallen out onto the newspaper spread out over the kitchen table where I took great delight in squashing them with the back of my thumbnail.

Teddy Burrows I'd been sitting by, I recalled. A dirty lot, the Burrows, Mam had always maintained and she'd warned me to keep as far away as possible from Teddy in case I caught another lot.

"There's kind of you and Mrs. Evans. It really is," Mrs. Williams sighed as she sat and gazed at the bundle of clothes I'd placed in her arms, unable for the moment to find her lap. "Really lovely they'll look." And I felt a momentary pang of guilt as I looked around at the pathetic silent circle, realising that it would never have occured to me to give any clothes to them at all if it hadn't furthered my own ends.

"Sorry you've caught us in a bit of a muddle Mr. Evans," she apologised as I thankfully lifted the latch to make my escape. "But the kids had just come home from school for their tea, and there's so much to do, what with my Sid being away and all . . ." I assured her that I quite understood and hurriedly made my exit, taking great appreciative gulps of fresh air as I crunched my way through the weeds and cockle shells to the Dago Joneses. But the sound of my name made me stop and turn and there was Mrs. Williams hurrying after me.

"Give this to Mrs. Evans now, for the clothes you know. I made it myself only last week." and she thrust a sticky dark jar of blackberry jam into my hand. The label said Strawberry and the pale red crust remaining around the rim gave proof of its original contents. I thanked her effusively for her kind offer, while thinking what the hell I was going to do with it, as the thought of actually eating anything cooked in that crowded, odorous room made me shudder as I tapped cautiously on the second paint-starved door.

"She's in," Mrs. Williams assured me, beaming, "I just saw her come back up the path from the lav . . . we shares it see."

"Thank you," I smiled back weakly, forcibly restraining an almost uncontrollable desire to scratch my head.

The latch lifted and the door opened. My throat suddenly went dry and I stood there foolishly holding out Pa's flannel suit as Mrs. Dago Jones wiped her hands on her sacking apron and stared at me with her deep, dark eyes, while Mrs. Williams, Dull Reggie and the rest of her bedraggled brood congregated on the dried mud patch and watched the proceedings with curious, silent interest.

"Mr. Evans has just popped up with some clothes," volunteered Mrs. Williams, shifting her babe from one hip to the other. "That grey will look a treat on your Dago."

Mrs. Dago Jones opened the door wider and nodded me inside with a canny look which made me feel that she could read my mind.

The room had an earth floor, the same as next door. The smoky air was heavy with the thick, cloying-sweet smell from the warm. bloody entrails of two freshly gutted rabbits stretched furry grey and glassy eyed on the table before me. By the meagre light filtering in through the small, dirty laced windows I could just make out the small crumpled bundle of clothes encasing the meagre figure of Dago Jones fast asleep in the high backed windsor chair by the grate, his feet out-stretched to the fire where a bubbling pan quietly hiss-spitted onto the coals beneath.

"This is your Pa's." declared Mrs. Jones, slushing her s's juicily as she always did as she held the grey flannel suit aloft.

"Well . . . yes . . ." I agreed. "We've been having a bit of a clear out, you see . . ." I explained for the second time. "I thought it would be just right for Dago there. Nice bit of cloth it is mind. And Myra sent up a few things for you . . ." I trailed off, handing over the remainder of my charitable offerings.

She put the clothes down on a chest of drawers without a word, and picking up a wickedly honed knife from the table she swiftly severed the feet from the luckless rabbits and whipped them out of their skins with a rapidity which made my eyes blink.

The spitting water hissed, Dago snored gently and I cleared my throat noisily as I desperately tried to think of a way to broach the subject of her medicines.

Mrs. Dago Jones finished her task with a swift double decapitation before gesturing to a chair with the stained knife and sitting herself down on the opposite side of the bloody table.

"Th . . . thank you Mrs. Jones," I stammered, taking the proferred seat. Her dark canny eyes stared at me from her swarthy, lined face and I carefully placed Mrs. Williams' pot of blackberry jam before me on the table.

"Mrs. Williams made it," I explained apologetically, with a nervous grin.

"How's your Mam?"

Thankful for the opening, I went into graphic details of how Mam was, how she liked living with her sister and . . .

"I always liked your Mam." she interrupted, leaning back in her chair and suddenly appearing more friendly disposed towards me. "And what can I do for you, Evan Evans?" she said quietly, eyeing me with a curious smile on her lips.

Again I had the uncomfortable impression that she knew why I was there and I felt like banging the table and shouting . . . You know damn well what you can do for me! But instead I found myself saying politely,

"Well, funny you should mention Mam, because you remember all the medicines you used to make for me when I was a kid?"

She nodded. "Yes, yes," she slushed, making little drops of glistening spittle at the corners of her mouth.

"Well . . . I was wondering . . . you see . . ."

"Five years it is since you wed your Myra, isn't it?" she asked pointedly.

"Well, that's just it, you see . . ." I hinted, leaning confidentially over the table and taking a quick wary look round at old Dago. After all, I didn't want him listening and spreading it all over The Prince when he was blotto.

"I was just wondering if there was anything in your . . . er . . . mixtures . . . that might have . . . you know . . . affected me now . . . or . . . " I dwindled off lamely. "Bromide perhaps?" I ventured tentatively.

Mrs. Dago Jones gave a chuckle. "There's no bromide up there, Evan Evans!" And I followed her eyes up to find dozens of dried plants and herbs hanging in clusters from the sooty old beams.

"Ah . . . yes . . . no . . . of course . . ." I faltered. "So, you don't think that . . .?"

"Seven he's given me." She announced, jerking her head over at poor old Dago who didn't look as if he'd ever had the strength to lift a petticoat leave alone anything else.

"All gone back on the road," she sighed, "Willy and Joe in Ireland and God knows where the rest is."

"Indeed," I murmured politely.

"And seven you shall have if you wants them!"

"Well, just one or two would do," I hurriedly assured her. "More medicine, is it?" I asked, raising my eyes to the crowded ceiling.

Again that chuckle bubbled over.

"The Sea, Evan Evans! The Sea will give them to you, boy!"

Fascinated, I watched the spittle bubbles form and burst as she juicily uttered the enigmatic advice.

She pushed the pink, slithery rabbits away and leant towards me. I waited expectantly for the recipe for my future virility, my heart pounding in my ears, my fingers convulsively clutching at Mrs. Williams's pot of blackberry jam.

"The Sea!" I repeated, slowly, half hypnotised.

Her black eyes narrowed.

"Shrimps is good," she whispered.

I nodded. "Shrimps is good," I echoed.

"Mussels is magnificent!" she said a little louder and my eyes opened wider.

"But oysters," she roared, "is bloody unbelievable!" and old Dago noisily choked himself on a startled snore.

"But . . ." and her voice dropped back to a whisper, "but, cockles is convenient," she finished on a matter of fact tone.

"Cockles is very convenient," I agreed, nodding my head fervently.

Suddenly I recalled the thousands of empty cockle shells I'd crunched my way over outside both cottages. Fifteen children between the two of them they had, not counting the numerous ones Dull Reggie's Pa had sired in Carmarthen.

"A few now and again is not a damn bit of good, mind," she warned, moving over to the bubbling pan on the fire. "Pack a year's eating into one month you must, Evan Evans," she cautioned, "and you'll soon see the results of the Food of the Sea! Grand it'll be . . . real grand!" She lifted the heavy pan onto the table. The salty smell of the sea filled my nostrils as I leant over and peered into the steamy depths.

Cockles!

Hundreds of cockles, each with its bright yellow foot poking from its gaping shell.

By damn I was full by the time I got up from the table fifteen minutes later! I reckoned I'd sunk my teeth into the rubbery flesh of at least two hundred, and when I'd finished I'd stared in disbelief at the mountain of empty cockle shells at my elbow. Not a speck of salt nor a drop of vinegar had she let me put on them. Acid kills their potency she'd warned as I'd gulped down the neat cockles and the two mugs of home-brewed ginger beer she'd poured for me.

"Champagne and oysters it's supposed to be, but cockles and ginger beer will do you just as well," she'd maintained, "You've just got to swallow twice as much, that's all!"

"Thank you very much indeed, Mrs. Jones," I belched, as I made my way to the door. A real explosion it was—would even have done old Lloyd the Stationmaster justice, fair play.

"Twice a day, mind!" she warned as she followed me through the door, her sacking apron full of empty cockle shells.

"Twice a day, Mrs. Jones," I repeated fervently, tucking Mrs. Williams's jar of jam into one pocket and another jar of ready shelled cockles into the other.

"Give your Mam my love, Evan Evans!" she called, noisily scattering the empty shells over the neglected garden.

I raised my hand in acknowledgement as I crunched my way back to the road with a heavy stomach but a light heart, determined to find that whip and top as soon as I reached home.

Chapter 6

"Not for breakfast, surely Evan!" Myra admonished as I tipped the contents of Mrs. Dago Jones's jam-jar into a basin before me the following morning.

"Well, 'twice a day', she said," I reminded her, "Guaranteed to stop you catching cold all the winter—provided you eat enough in the autumn . . . must be something like cod liver oil, I suppose." I lied, smilingly.

"But you never do have a cold, Evan!" Myra insisted with a mystified shake of her head.

"Ah . . . but it's going to be a hard winter this year . . . very hard," I pointed out. "You should see the hedges, covered with berries they are. That's a sure sign." And I tucked into my cockle breakfast with relish. "You may as well have a few yourself," I suggested, pushing the basin across the kitchen table.

Gingerly she picked up a fat, juicy cockle and squelched it between her teeth.

"I think I'll have some at tea-time," she promised as she forced the solitary cockle down with a determined gulp. "I don't really fancy them for breakfast."

"No need to tell anyone about it, mind," I warned, between mouthfuls. "We don't want them to think that we take any notice of what old Dago Jones's Missus tells us, after all."

Myra nodded in agreement as she poured another strong cup of tea, her eyes watching me with admiration as I shovelled in the cockles.

"I'll get some more fresh ones early this afternoon," I proposed, pushing the empty dish away with a replete sigh of satisfaction. "The tide'll be low then. A bucket full should last us for a couple of days, I should think . . . and, by the way, could you get a couple of bottles of ginger beer from Lewis the Grocer?"

She opened her eyes wide. "But you don't like ginger beer!" she exclaimed.

"Ah . . . well . . . no," I reluctantly agreed, "But Mrs. Dago Jones said that the ginger helps to keep the warmth in the body. And I'll need it if I'm helping old Dai on a bit of outside work this winter. All helps to stop you catching cold, you see."

"All right then," she agreed, giving a quick look up at the

clock. "Come on, Evan," she hurried, "Time to pull up the blinds. You don't want me in the shop this morning, do you love?" she asked as she started to clear away the dishes.

"No, no," I assured her, giving the back of her neck a swift kiss as I followed her out into the back kitchen with the kettle of hot water. "You please your little self what ever you want to do, my lovely." I smiled, giving her a squeeze.

"Oh, Evan! The blinds, mind," she giggled.

Oh, by damn, Mrs. Dago Jones was right about those cockles, I thought elatedly as I made my way into the dark shop, humming happily to myself.

As the blinds went up the bulky outline of Dull Reggie, sporting my old green pullover, slowly came into view. I gave him a wave through the glass, and slowly he waved back.

Mrs. Nellie Williams's youngest was standing outside the door, I noticed, as I drew back the bolts. She pushed open the door and stood politely before me.

"What can I do for you then, Jenny?" I smiled, bending down on my haunches to be on her level.

"Mr. Jenkins said," she lisped, "would you please send Dull Reggie to school. He hasn't been for two days and I said I knew where he was."

"Right you are, my dear," I laughed. "You come along with me then," and out we both went onto the pavement.

"School, Reggie!" I said, slowly and clearly, catching hold of his arm and turning him gently away from the fascinations of Alice and Maud.

He stared at me blankly.

"School today." I insisted, turning him round further and giving him a slight push in the right direction.

"'I must work hard'!" I reminded him as he reluctantly started to shuffle off, his head twisted round to take a last lingering look at the shop window.

"See he gets past Lewis the Ironmonger's window!" I called after little Jenny who was skipping off up the hill.

"Come on, Reggie," she ordered, retracing her steps and taking hold of his short thick fingers. And off the pair of them went—dainty little Jenny with her obedient lumbering giant at her side. What the hell Ann Thomas was going to do with him all day, I couldn't imagine as I went back into the shop and started dusting down the counter ready for the day's customers.

It was half past one when I set out for the beach, kitted out in my old gardening clothes and wellington boots. I had been Dressed for Drapery for two days and really unshackled I felt as I strode purposefully down the hill, my empty bucket and sawn-off rake swinging at my side.

Gradually I found myself catching up with the stout bustling figure of Mrs. Nellie Williams who was hurrying on her daily trip down to the Signal Box with her Billie's basin of steaming hot broth.

"'Afternoon, Mrs. Williams," I greeted as I reached her side.

"Oh, hello, Mr. Evans," she replied, a bit out of breath. "A nice drop of salt beef I've got for Billie's dinner today," she confided, giving the enormous plate covered basin in her basket a loving pat. "And a nice bit of bread pudding," she added.

"Smells lovely," I said with an appreciative sniff.

"Just off for a bit of cockling, are you Mr. Evans?" she asked, noticing my apparel and equipment.

"Well, Myra fancied a few, you know," I explained, guiltily.

"I hear you and Mrs. Evans gave Dull Reggie's Mam and Mrs. Dago Jones some of your old clothes yesterday." she went on. "There's kind of you both." she beamed.

Mrs. L. Y. T. Jones had obviously wasted no time in spreading the news, I thought with an inward smile as I stepped out, leaving the puffing Mrs. Williams behind me.

A very gratifying experience, cockling, and the next hour sped swiftly away as I scraped and raked my back-aching, solitary way across the expanse of exposed mud, rock and seaweed. My bucket gradually grew heavy as I picked the harvest of the low tide and it was with a sigh of satisfaction that I finally straightened my back and tramped back up the beach, my future fertility assured in the brimming bucket of shells at my side.

"How's it going, then, Dai?" I called in through the cement store door, placing the heavy bucket down by the doorpost. "How did you get on with my Tabitha on Wednesday night then?"

He paused in his task of stacking the hefty bags and straightened himself up with a grateful sigh.

"Tabitha?" he echoed, looking puzzled as he wiped the sweat and cement dust off his face.

"You know—the model." I reminded him.

"Oh . . . her," he answered as light dawned. "Oh, great, man. They all thought it was a grand idea—paid up a penny each, no trouble at all." and he pushed his hand into the back pocket of his overalls and handed over Tabitha's first wages. "Here's your two bob." And he dropped a handful of pennies and halfpennies into my hand.

"Ideal, she was. One of the best Ambulance Practices we've had." he went on as he dusted himself down. "Bit of luck her arms coming off—we could pass 'em round for a bit of individual bandaging. Davis the Coal did a grand Figure of Eight on her elbow. I tell you boy, by the end of the meeting she'd been bandaged for more accidents than I've had cooked dinners! Young Umshla was a bit beetroot, mind, 'til he got used to her . . . first time he's ever handled the female form, I reckon!" He leant up against the pile of cement bags and grinned at the recollection. "I must say, though, I did a real lovely hip spica bandage on her. I've never had those reverse spiral turns look so pretty . . . and P.C. Llewellyn did a grand job of splinting her fractured pelvis—give him his due, after all." Dai fished out a squashed dog-end from his pocket and lit up. He inhaled appreciatively. "Definitely. Your Tabitha was definitely a success," he avowed. And I listened with a delighted ear.

"You're looking a bit of a mess, aren't you?" he remarked, eyeing my mudcaked boots as we made our way across the yard to the Coffin Shed for a cup of tea. "What you been up to, then?"

I pointed to the shell filled bucket. "Myra fancied a few cockles," I explained, dispelling any notion that Dai might have that it was anything to do with me. I pushed open the door and looked round the wood cluttered shed. "Where is she, then?" I asked as I peered into the empty emergency coffin for Tabitha.

Dai pumped the primus vigorously.

"I've done you a bit of good, boy. You'll have to start giving me a bit of commission, I reckon."

"Oh? How's that?" I asked, really intrigued.

"Well, the Ambulance section over at Glynmawr heard about her from young Alan Webb the fireman. And they decided they'd like to hire her for practices as well, so I dropped her off at the British Legion Hut at Glynmawr when I went to fetch the cement from Haverfordwest this morning. She's coming back with Alan on the footplate of the 11.30 Goods tonight."

The primus spluttered and flared.

"Well, I'll be damned!" I marvelled as I handed him the pricker. "Glynmawr of all places."

"She's well wrapped up for travelling, like you suggested," he assured me, "so she won't be seen—or get dirty on the engine." His expert pricking was rewarded by a powerful roar as the primus burst into life. "Young Alan'll drop her off in here on his way home tonight—real organised it is."

"Well, I'll be damned," I repeated, "That's four bob a week she'll be making!"

"Don't forget my commission," Dai reminded with a grin. "Two pints at The Prince every Tuesday after Choir!"

"You're on, boy." I agreed without hesitation.

"Can't understand why you don't join the St. John's Ambulance, Evan," he reflected, carefully placing the can of water over the hissing blue flame.

"I reckon I've got enough common sense to cope with any emergency, boy," I retorted. "Look at that time when we went to that fight at Harford." I reminded him.

Back in the early spring it had been, with middleweights Sid Griffiths and Eric Hughes topping the bill at The Market House. Damn good boxers they were, both of them, and tickets for the match had been in such great demand that we'd failed to get any.

But Dai, Alf the Lion and myself had decided to go anyway, just on speck, to see if we could get in. And off we'd set with Alf in the sidecar and me on the pillion of Dai's bike. Alf had blankly refused to ride pillion—a bit scared he was. Mind you, he had every right to be—he was so damn frail and skinny that he'd probably have been blown away! Well when we'd eventually roared up Haverfordwest Hill, nearly scaring poor old Alf out of his wits as we'd heeled round the steep corner up to the Market House, we'd been a bit dismayed to find a gang of local chaps already crowding round the door, all hoping to buy a bit of standing room at the back, like us.

"It's bloody useless, man." Dai had grumbled as we'd stood at the edge of the crowd. "We can't get near the entrance leave alone get in." Really disappointed we were.

"Well, let's have a go, at least," I'd suggested, "as we've come this far."

Over the next half hour we surreptitiously managed to infiltrate ourselves into the crowd. But then we seemed to get stuck and any further progress was barred by a group of hefty chaps who obviously would stand no messing.

"Only quarter of an hour it is before the fight starts," announced Dai glumly as we stood there, wedged shoulder to shoulder, cupping our fags protectively in our hands.

We eyed the lucky ticket holders enviously as they marched confidently past the jostling crowd and squeezed themselves in through the doorway. Maddening it was—so near and yet so far.

Then disaster struck! The excitement and crush suddenly overwhelmed poor old Alf the Lion and he slumped down between us, clean out like a light.

"Bloody hell!" gasped Dai in real consternation as we tried to hold up Alf's sagging little body which was threatening to disappear under the tangle of feet.

"Fresh air!" he shouted. "A man's fainted over by 'ere!" All his St. John's Ambulance training came to the fore as he made to push a way out to the edge of the crowd with the limp body, nobly abandoning all hopes of seeing the best middleweight boxing match of the year in his dedication to the Hypocratic tradition.

"This way you bloody fool!" I hissed in his ear as I grabbed hold of Alf's other arm and pulled them both in the direction of the door. Alf continued to sag alarmingly. "Up over our heads with him," I ordered and up over our heads Alf's feather light body went. The crowd jostled and murmured in sympathy around us.

"Give him room to breathe!" I yelled.

"Fresh air!" Demanded Dai, urgently.

"Let us through please," I shouted up to those at the front of the queue who were still ignorant of the commotion further back.

"St. John's Ambulance," I proclaimed with great authority. "A man's fainted. Let us through please." And a pathway opened up to the door like Moses dividing the sea and in to the entrance hall we staggered with Alf over our heads, and Dai still demanding "Fresh Air!" and nobody thinking how dull it was to carry a man into a hot, stuffy building in order to get it!

By damn it was a good fight too! A knock-out in the tenth round—and Alf the Lion watched it all from a ringside seat found for him by a sympathetic official who feared, from Alf's frail appearance, that he might faint again if he had to stand throughout the fight!

I shook the packet of tea generously into the can of steaming water and winked across at Dai.

"Like I said—common sense you want as well as your old St. John's Ambulance." and he grinned back as he took my point.

"How are you getting on with your Ann Thomas, then?" I asked, giving the can of tea a strengthening stir.

"Oh . . . she's lovely man. I brought her up to see my new piece of land yesterday evening. I tell you, as long as I don't hear any more from Sybil over at The Farmer's I'll be the happiest man in Wales."

"I suppose you'll be leaving your ladder in the Tugwell's backyard soon then?" I grinned.

He looked at me askance. "Never boy! Nothing like that . . . pure she is. And she thinks I'm a real gentleman!"

I let out a guffaw of disbelief.

"No, really now . . . I've turned over a new leaf. Nothing's going to spoil it, see? She's the one for me, boy." And he stubbed his cigarette out determinedly on the side of the glue pot.

"You'll be taking her to the Church Whistdrive Supper and Dance tomorrow night then?" I asked.

"That's a damn fine idea, Evan. I hadn't thought of that. Then off to the Bleeding Tree on Sunday—a lovely weekend it'll be."

Our tea drunk, we sauntered out into the yard once more where Dai eyed his mud-splattered motor-bike and sidecar with a critical eye.

"I'll have to give it a bit of a clean up before I take Ann to

Nevern," he observed, running his finger through a layer of dust on the sidecar windscreen.

"Oh aye," I agreed, "must keep up the good impression!"

I picked up my rake and bucket of cockles and turned to leave.

"By the way, Evan . . ." I stopped in my tracks. "Can you give me a hand up at the Captain's place next Monday? I fetched those damn stones out of Tut-Tut's boat yesterday," he went on, "and took two loads up to Tŷ Mawr on the lorry. They're just dumped inside his drive, so if you could . . ."

"All right, boy," I agreed.

"Hey," Dai recollected with a grin, "There's a lovely little thing that daughter of his has turned out! That Selina!" and he undulated his hands expressively in the air.

"Dai Rees!" I cautioned, as the old familiar twinkle gleamed in his eye.

"A gentleman I said I was going to be—not a bloody monk, man!"

And I left him giving the sidecar a bit of a speculative rub up as a sudden breeze sent the grey cement dust swirling round his feet.

*   *   *

"Oh, there you are," greeted Myra as I sat in the back kitchen heaving off my mud-caked boots. "I hoped you'd be home soon."

"Why love? What's the matter? Do you need a bit of a hand in the shop?"

"No, no, tidily busy I am. No, it's just that Bertie James the carriage cleaner popped in not five minutes ago to see if you would go down for a bit of choir practice with Umshla." she explained.

"I'll keep these on then," I said, pushing my feet back into my boots and getting up to go. "Not worth my while Dressing for Drapery if you can manage for the rest of the afternoon, is it? I'll just wash the cockles and leave them to spit before I go."

"All right, love," she said, giving a peck of a kiss on the end of my nose, then off she flew back into the shop as the distant ping heralded another customer.

Quickly I poured half a can of water over the muddy shells,

pushed up my sleeve and plunged my arm into the bucket, rattling the cockles round until they were clean. Carefully I tipped the dirty water away on the garden, scattered a handful of salt over the clean shells and refilled the bucket to the brim with clean water, leaving them to open slowly and spit out any grit they might have collected.

"I'll fetch more water when I come back," I called through the passage and I placed the two cans by the back door to remind me.

The strains of 'Thanks be to God! He laveth the thirsty land', guided me to the particular carriage Umshla had chosen for his choir practice that particular day. The coach stood, along with a few others in the siding, on the far side of the station yard. I jumped down from the platform where Umshla's watering can, hoe and spade lay momentarily neglected for higher things, and crossed the lines towards the soaring melodic sounds.

I heaved myself up at the open door at the end of the carriage, carefully avoiding an out-size cleaners' brush and a long length of hose snaking in through the door from a gas point alongside the track outside. Our local coaches were regularly berthed in these sidings for re-fuelling as the compartments were lit by gas, unlike the mainline coaches which had the ultra refinement of electric lights.

But old Bertie James the cleaner had long ago discovered a highly unorthodox, but very effective use for the compressed gas . . . Blew it down the lavatories he did! And I would guarantee that the Llanporth coaches had the cleanest lavs on the G.W.R., for nothing could resist that powerful jet as it roared down the pan and out the other end.

"Busy?" I called sociably as I looked in the tiny cubicle at the bent back of old Bertie James who was merrily blowing the lav clean.

He looked up in surprise. "Nearly finished this one Evan, boy," he assured me, seemingly quite unaware of the strong smell of gas which left me momentarily gasping. "Umshla's lot is down by there in the middle compartment—the Non-smoker," he advised as he returned to his breath-taking task.

And sure enough, there in the Third Class Non-smoker I found Fred Harris, along with two other G.W.R. tenors, sitting facing Young Umshla, all wreathed in blue Woodbine smoke, their music copies held high as they warbled their way through the long Amen.

I slid open the door and poked my head in.

"C . . . c . . . come . . . come in and sh . . . sh . . . shut the d . . . d . . . d . . . damn d . . . d . . . door," ordered Umshla. "b . . . bl . . . bloomin' B . . . B . . . Bertie would have to g . . . g . . . go and cl . . . clean out his bl . . . bl . . . bloomin' l . . . l . . . lavs right n . . . nn . . . now." he grumbled. "B . . . b . . . bloomin' awful smell of g . . . g . . . gas everywhere."

I did as I was bid, took a copy of Zardok off the seat and sat down with the others.

"Umshall . . . umshall . . . um shall we take it from the fifth bar, b . . . boys? And a n . . . nn . . . nice sw . . . sw . . . swell on 'relief' now." Expertly he flicked his tuning fork on the window framing, hummed a few experimental doh, me, sohs, and sang "Take this note!"

We all took it.

"After three," he intoned, still on the note like a monk at evensong. I opened my mouth, took a deep breath . . . and found myself hurtling across the compartment as an almighty explosion ripped through the carriage. Glass shattered round us and the sound of splintering wood filled the air. Copies of Zardok floated around like autumn leaves and Umshla's tuning fork disappeared under the seat.

Dazedly I picked myself up from the floor as the remaining tenors of the Llanporth Choir staggered about choking and gasping.

"What the bloody hell was that?" coughed Fred, staring about bemused. I frantically fumbled to open the door and we all fell out over each other onto the track below to see old Bertie James, his face black and his clothes torn staggering dazedly towards us like a drunken Bishop.

"I thought you lot was in a Non-smoker!" he shouted, pointing an accusing finger at us stunned songsters.

"It wasn't us, man!" retorted Fred, struggling to his feet. "The damn explosion was down your end!"

We all stared, flabbergasted, at the wrecked end of the coach and old Bertie shook his head, utterly perplexed as to how, after fifteen years of uneventful lav-gassing, his unique cleaning method could suddenly have blown up on him.

"It's never bloody happened before!" he muttered sadly as he viewed the debris strewn over the track.

"B . . . b . . . better get b . . . b . . . back to work, b . . . b . . . boys," stammered Umshla as he attempted to gather up his precious music copies from the glass shattered compartment and from our clutching hands. "S . . . s . . . same time t . . . t . . . tomorrow," he suggested as we all staggered away in various directions, leaving Bertie scratching his head as he tried to think of a reasonable story to tell Lloyd the Stationmaster.

"Had a good practice, love?" Myra asked as I wandered shakily in through the back door, the salty steam from the boiling cockles billowing in my face as I tried to clear my throat to answer.

I giggled stupidly.

"We got blown up!" I announced, my voice rising to an uncontrollable squeak of almost hysterical laughter as I recalled the stunned look of utter disbelief on poor old Bertie's blackened face.

"Oh well, never mind," she commented, not grasping the full implication of what I had said as she busily gave her attention to ladling out the steaming cockles. "Come and have your cockles, quick love," she said as the last few particles of inhaled G.W.R. compartment dust tickled my nose into a gargantuan sneeze "because it sounds as if you've caught a cold after all . . .!"

Chapter 7

"We've done really well in the shop this week, Myra," I announced with some satisfaction as I sat back after having added up the takings the following evening. I always liked to do a quick total up of the week's accounts as soon as the blinds came down on a Saturday night, and this week we had broken all records.

"You sold a good bit today then, Evan," she remarked as she looked over my shoulder at the healthily balanced page of accounts.

"Why aye, girl . . . changed Alice and Maud twice I did, mind," I said with some pride.

Myra hadn't been in the shop all day. It was her turn to provide the trifles and Welsh-cakes for the monthly Whistdrive Supper and Dance which was being held in the Church Hall that night and she'd been busy in the kitchen since early morning.

An extra gridle had been borrowed from Susie Webb next door and the delicious spicy aroma of gently browning Welsh-cakes had filtered in to the shop right through the day, for no sooner was one batch cooked when Myra was up to her elbows in flour and fruit again with another mixture. The three enormous bowls from the wash-stand sets upstairs had been rinsed and filled with steaming red, green and yellow jellies poured over the Tugwells' stale cake, and left to set out the back and by six o'clock the sideboard was laden with mountains of mouthwatering Welsh-cakes and wobbling jellies, their colourful hues now hidden under layers of cherry and angelica decorated blancmange and cream.

Really artistic Myra was when it came to decorating a trifle, I thought as I pushed the account book into the sideboard drawer and dipped an experimental finger in the cream and gave it an appreciative lick.

"Tea's ready!"

I turned from the tempting array with keen anticipation.

"Cockles," she said brightly as she sat herself down behind the teapot. "And ginger beer," she added as she placed the glass of gaseous fluid before me with a flourish before sitting back to sip her own cup of strong sweet tea appreciatively.

Aw hell, I thought despondently, my face falling as I stared at the uncompromising dishful of cold shell-fish. I had to admit that my enthusiasm was definitely beginning to wane as I resignedly forked up half a dozen circles of grey and yellow flesh and set to to plod my way through the remainder, determined to have my necessary rations before indulging myself with a single Welsh-cake.

I gulped the last one down with the help of the fizzy ginger beer and thanked God that I wouldn't have to face another of the yellow-footed little beasts until tomorrow.

*   *   *

"The copper's nearly on the boil!" Myra called through from the back kitchen as I followed her out with the rest of the dirty dishes.

"We'll have to hurry, mind, or we'll be late," she warned as she bustled past me to give the tablecloth a shake outside the back door.

"Come and get the bath in, Evan love."

I pushed a few more sticks under the boiler and went outside.

"Who's going to have it first this week, then?" she asked as I reached up to unhook the heavy galvanized bath off the wall and staggered back into the kitchen with its unwieldly shape.

"You can if you like, love," I offered as we both set to ladling out the steaming water from the stone built copper in the corner.

"Dast, we'll have to be quick," she fretted, with another anxious look at the clock. "Mrs. Rees-Williams likes the jellies and Welsh-cakes to be there early so that she can arrange the tables nicely." Mrs. Rees-Williams never indulged in any of the actual hard work of preparing the food for The Supper—only directed the artistic arranging of the tables when the ladies of Llanporth arrived with the provisions. This week Mrs. Lloyd was cutting all the bread and butter and Ann Thomas had offered to help Mrs. L. Y. T. Jones clean the potatoes. Cy the Butcher was boiling a ham, as usual. He always provided a ham or tongue a bit cheaper for the Whistdrive, Supper and Dance, as it was paid for out of the money collected from the twopence ha'penny kitty. And Mrs. Rees-Williams supervised it all. A dab hand with a paper doily and a carnation was Mrs. Rees-Williams, fair play.

We continued to splash the necessary amount of water into the waiting bath, with Myra still fretting about how quick we'd have to be, when to my astonishment I heard myself saying, "Let's have a bath together, then—save time it will!"

The idea had never occurred to me before, and even then, I had to be quite honest with myself and admit that it wasn't really the consideration of saving time which made me suggest it at that precise moment!

"Evan!" Myra gasped, askance, pushing a stray, damp curl back from her flushed face—and, by damn, there's pretty she looked too, with the steam swirling about and the glowing firelight flickering around.

My ladling speeded up as my fervour increased.

"I'll fetch the towels," Myra offered, giving silent acquiescence to my suggestion and within seconds two large, fluffy towels were spread out in front of the fire to warm.

On reflection it must have been a tight squeeze for the two of us in that narrow zinc bath, but I can't say that I noticed it, and it didn't save us any time at all—in fact, that particular Saturday bath-time took longer than it had ever done! Much later, as we lay contentedly outstretched before the fire on the thick, warm towels my hand closed over something hard and round. I held it up in the firelight and a stray, empty cockle shell glinted back at me. I closed my fingers over it gratefully and turned to give Myra a long appreciative kiss.

"Did the hot water soak that nasty old splinter out of your knee, Evan?" she asked as she idly twirled her fingers through my hair.

I looked.

It had.

*   *   *

The green baize tables were already in position around the hall with Davis the Coal expertly flicking open four folding chairs at each one when Myra and I eventually arrived. Umshla Watkins was up the step ladder fixing a bit of bunting which had drooped sadly since the last festivities a month ago and Mrs. Rees-Williams stood in the doorway of The Supper Room impatiently fluttering her sheaf of paper doilies.

"At last, Mrs. Evans!" she rebuked sharply, rustling forward in her shot-blue taffeta and long pearls to examine the contents of the large wicker clothes basket we carried between us. Damned heavy it had been, too, what with the three washstand basins of trifle, the couple of hundred Welsh-cakes, Myra's pale blue satin dance slippers and my black patent shoes.

We staggered into The Supper Room with our contribution and set it down on the floor with a thankful sigh. The long trestle tables were already draped with vast shroudlike white tablecloths and laid with an assortment of knives, forks and spoons. Single carnations, especially selected from Captain Rees-Williams's greenhouse stood elegantly, with a spray of asparagus fern, in the loaned silver-plated flower vases and the thick, Sunday School cups and saucers sat stolidly grouped at the end of each table.

"There aren't any silver balls!" Mrs. Rees-Williams observed in consternation as I lifted the decorated trifles out one by one. Myra had meant to pop round to Lewis the Shop's back door for some after we'd got ready, but our unaccustomed bathtime activities had put it clean out of her head!

"Silver balls do set off my silver plate so well!" she vexed. Myra opened her mouth to apologise for the omission when I interrupted with "Well, Mrs. Rees-Williams, we'd heard a few complaints about people nearly breaking their teeth on them, so Myra thought angelica and cherries would be safer . . ."

Mrs. Rees-Williams sniffed disdainfully and flashed her be-ringed hands in a wave of dismissal as she set about arranging the Welsh-cakes on her doilies with a sigh of one sorely tried.

I gave Myra a wink and we made our way over to the hooks to hang up our coats and hats.

By half past seven the main hall was crowded with chattering groups of gossiping, laughing townsfolk, all dressed up to the nines and happily anticipating a good night out. Myra stood on tip-toe and whispered in my ear, "I keep seeing Alice and Maud wherever I look!" she giggled, and by damn, she was right for at least seven of the Llanporth ladies were sporting their 'model' frocks for the first time! Each one eyeing the others and effusing how marvellous they all looked.

Mind you, some of the frocks had lost a bit of style and looked quite different now that they were encompassing a League 3 or 4 figure, but the wearers confidently saw themselves as appearing just as elegant as the models in my shop window, so that was all that mattered. All except Mrs. Ruby Tyler, that is. She filled that brown silk better than any plaster model could. The long, beaded fringe swung provocatively round her slim, pink-stockinged knees with every movement and . . .

A playful finger tickled my ribs.

"I know what you're thinking!"

I looked away guiltily. "Oh . . ." I stammered.

"The spitting image of Alice she is in that dress, isn't she? Look at the way she holds her hand and everything . . ."

"Yes indeed, you're quite right," I laughed weakly.

"Just as if Alice had come to life, it is!" Myra went on. I remembered those slender arms slowly melting round my neck and a shiver went down my spine.

"Dai's late!" I said loudly, changing the subject. Myra looked round the hall.

"I saw Ann Thomas arrive ten minutes ago with the potatoes. I think she must still be in The Supper Room, but I haven't seen Dai at all," she puzzled.

There was no more time to wonder what could be keeping Dai, however, as Jenkins the Schoolmaster was already blowing his whistle and directing everybody to take their places at the tables. Myra and I sauntered over to Table 5 and I beckoned to Ann, who stood hesitating at the Supper Room doorway, to join us.

"Has Mr. Dai Rees arrived yet?" she asked, gazing round the room.

"I can't understand it," I replied, passing over the pencil for her to write her name on the score card. "He's always here for The Whist."

The last few loners wandered about filling up any spaces at the tables and Umshla Watkins halted by our empty chair. His eyes avoided looking at either Ann or Myra and he shuffled his heavy G.W.R. boots selfconsciously.

"Umshla, umshla, um . . . um shall . . . Um . . . shall I sit by 'ere?" he stammered, his face turning beetroot red as his downcast eyes stared fixedly at his watch-chain. There's a difference from his self assurance when he was taking choir practice down in the sidings, I thought, sympathising with his obvious embarrassment. Take a choral sheet or a garden fork out of his hands and put him within ten feet of a woman and the poor chap went to pieces. But fair play, he was a good whist player—once he'd found somewhere to sit and had a fistful of cards to focus his attention on.

I gave a last quick look in the direction of the door but there was still no sign of the elusive Dai, so I assured Umshla that we'd all be delighted to have him join us.

Myra cleared her throat politely. "I hear your Mam has been called away to her brother's in Pontypridd."

Umshla nodded as he took his seat.

"Very bad, is he?"

He nodded once more, keeping his eyes firmly fixed on the pack of cards in the centre of the table as his fingers nervously fumbled with the St. John's Ambulance medallion swinging on his watch-chain.

I picked up the pack and shuffled the thickened, furry cards with difficulty. About time we bought some new ones, I thought, as I slapped them down for Umshla to cut.

All around us fags were being clipped out and pocketed, fingers were being flexed and spectacles adjusted in readiness for the commencement of play. We all looked round expectantly at the still vacant Table One with its untorn green baize and its slick, nearly-new pack of cards. Biding their time with the assurance of their indisputable position in the hierarchy of the town, Captain and Mrs. Rees-Williams and The Vicar and his wife eventually condescended to take their places at their customary Table One near the Tortoise stove. In the summer, mind you, Table One could always be found nearest the only window which would open. Very deferent we were in Llanporth, you see.

Myra gave a bit of a shiver and wrapped her new Spanish shawl more closely round her bare shoulders.

"I hope I keep winning," she said with a laugh, "then I can move up nearer the stove!" And we all agreed that it was a trifle chilly down our end.

At a signal from Captain Rees-Williams, Jenkins the

Schoolmaster put his whistle to his lips and blew. The Llanporth Church Whistdrive, Supper and Dance could officially begin.

For the next five minutes nothing could be heard except the slap of cards, the occasional discreet cough, the quiet bubbling of the first batch of potatoes boiling on the gas ring in The Supper Room and the rhythmic squeak of Old Jenkins's boots as he raised and lowered his heels while warming his broad behind at the glowing Tortoise stove. He kept a wary schoolmaster's eye on the proceedings and glowered at poor old Alf the Lion who came apologetically tip-toeing through the hall with the two extra cans of water for the tea, just as he did with any unfortunate pupil who dared to come late to school.

A murmur of voices started up as the first hand was completed.

"Seven to us, it is," I announced with some satisfaction as I collected up the last trick, won by my tactically saved trump card. It had been a tight game with Ann and Umshla partnering well, and we all congratulated each other on our standard of play as we filled in the score cards. Then Myra and I, as the winning pair, parted company and proceeded in opposite directions to the adjoining tables.

Only once in the next five hands did I lose and as I glanced across the room I could tell from the distance Myra had travelled towards the Tortoise stove that she, too, was having her fair share of success. I also could not help but notice that Mrs. Ruby Tyler and I were drawing inexorably closer, with each hand, and I was more determined to keep winning and keep moving.

"Good evening, partner," came that luscious, throaty greeting at last, as I sat myself down opposite her on Table 12. A narrow silver-plaited headband sat low on her forehead, Red Indian fashion, long jet earings dangled from those delicious pink lobes peeping from under her sleek, dark hair and a knowing smile played on her carmined lips.

"Er . . . good evening Mrs. Tyler," I replied, picking up the cards and giving them a violent shuffle which sent two of them skimming under the table. We both bent to retrieve them as the fuss of partners changing tables bustled about us. California Poppy filled my nostrils and sensually graphic images filled my mind.

"Did you hear about my damn old splinters?" she whispered under the table as her fingers reached for the Queen of Spades.

I nodded sympathetically—well, fair play, I did know what they felt like.

"Matthew's going to Fishguard again next Tuesday!"

My cockle filled stomach turned over with a lurch and my Come-to-Jesus collar suddenly grew uncomfortably tight as my blood pressure rocketed and my hand fumbled convulsively on the floor for the two of clubs. I waited for my mental warnings of 'Never again!' but somehow, in the back of my turmoiled mind, it was imperceptibly changing to 'Perhaps just once more!' I felt a fleeting pang of guilt, but after all, I reasoned, it was out of my control, wasn't it! It was the effect of all those damn cockles, they were the ones to blame. I mean, left up to the old me, it would never have happened in the first place—trapped I'd been, in Frankie Evans's guardsvan, left with no alternative. But, by damn, I felt a bit different about the offer this time—which proved that it was all due to Mrs. Dago Jones's cockle eating advice. I straightened myself up from under the table fully convinced that my new fate lay in my stomach and, as Old Lloyd the Stationmaster often pointed out when his own stomach erupted in an explosive burp, 'You can't defy the Laws of Nature'!

After all, if I wanted to produce a new owner for my whip and top that I'd successfully found up in the attic, I'd just have to risk these side effects!

Those lovely lips smiled amusedly across the green baize as I smoothed down my hair and tried to compose myself. Old Jenkins blew his whistle and announced trumps, Davis the Coal dealt the cards to us swiftly, a nervous Miss Gwendoline Davies gathered them secretly to her bosom while Mrs. Ruby Tyler splayed out her hand elegantly and I vainly tried to concentrate on whist.

I gazed at my hand blankly, my fingers automatically sorting the thirteen cards into suits. Gradually I became aware of three pairs of eyes on me. I blinked and focused my attention on the table where the Ace and three of spades lay waiting.

"Er . . . what was trumps?" I ventured, apologetically.

"Hearts!" murmured Ruby throatily.

I coughed nervously and scanned my hand, noticing, with

surprise, the complete lack of spades. Without thinking, I reached for the three of hearts and played it with a flourish. There was a swift, surprised intake of breath and Miss Gwendoline Daves threw away a deuce of spades, leaving me to pick up the trick.

"You just trumped your partner's Ace!" Davis the Coal declared loudly in unbelievable astonishment, his amazement making him forget to whisper. Heads turned in our direction and Jenkins the Schoolmaster shushed with annoyance as I felt my face grow hot with embarrassment. I whispered a profuse apology to Ruby, narrowed my eyes and made a supreme effort to concentrate on the game. But just as I was managing to think a little more clearly a gentle, nudging foot slowly started to caress my ankle and my whist went haywire again, leaving my mind in a turmoil of panic in case Old Jenkins spotted it and construed it as a form of signalling in order to cheat! To tell you the truth, I don't know which would have been the more damning—to have been accused of cheating at cards or of dallying with someone else's wife! And I didn't relish either.

Indeed now, trying to concentrate was useless and Davis the Coal and Gwendoline Davies picked up trick after trick. And there was me—a whist player who prided himself on remembering when each and every card was played, dithering over leading the Queen because, for the life of me, I couldn't remember whether the damn King had gone!

I lead.

It hadn't. And Gwendoline Davies produced it with triumphant delight, convinced that her somewhat dubious skill at Whist was definitely improving. I mean, sometimes she didn't move more than three tables all night, and had won the Booby Prize so many times that her kitchen must be filled with wooden spoons!

An unbelievable ten tricks to three we lost by and when Davis the Coal beamed, "Well played partner!" as he and Gwendoline rose to make the victors' walk to the next tables she blushed crimson with pure happiness. I could guarantee that she'd never had a ten on her score card before and I wouldn't have been a bit surprised if she'd framed it and hung it over the mantlepiece!

"Off form tonight then, Mr. Evans?" Ruby smiled as she

signed the check card. She looked up from under her silver Red Indian head band, her thinly pencilled eyebrows raised in teasing amusement.

"Not a bit of it, Mrs. Tyler," I heard myself reply. "Just got my mind on other things!" Now there's bold you must admit! There was no doubt about it, those damn cockles were definitely beginning to take effect.

"Move round then, Mr. Evans!" And there was Matthew Tyler waiting to partner Ruby for the next hand.

Mumbling a quick apology I changed my seat blowing my nose furiously in an attempt to hide my confusion and giving a nod of greeting to my new partner, Mrs. L. Y. T. Jones, who pushed her chair back a little to make room for her vast shelf of a bosom and announced, as she fixed a gimlet eye on me, that she hadn't lost a single hand so far.

She spoke too soon. Eight-five we lost by, but fair play, I did have the added distraction of a thinly stocking clad knee rubbing against my pinstripe trousers as well to contend with, although no-one would have guessed it by the sweetly efficient way Ruby partnered her husband. Damn she was cool—and lovely.

A dry old stick was Matthew Tyler, always smelt of T.C.P. —mind you, he looked very distinguished in his Customs and Exise uniform. It was probably that which had impressed Ruby in the first place, I thought, as I initialled the disastrous 8-5 score with a murmured apology to an irate Mrs. L. Y. T. Jones.

A very mediocre score I ended up with as you can imagine. Umshla Watkins won the Gents prize with Captain Rees Williams second and Jenkins the Schoolmaster's wife won the Ladies beating Mrs. L. Y. T. Jones by one point. And daggers she looked at me when the scores were finally read out! P.C. Llewellyn had the wooden spoon Booby prize and everybody congratulated a delighted Miss Gwendoline Davies on missing it, so it's an ill wind, I thought ruefully as I helped to move the chairs to the side of the hall and stack the whist tables behind the curtain before going outside to join the line of relieving male Llanporth whist players behind the old churchyard wall. Well, it wasn't worth trying to trample your way though the ferns and long grass to the official four-holer in the rickety old ivy-covered lean-to at the back of the hall. And there wasn't a glimmer of light in there to see what you were doing, and besides, it was an unspoken arrangement that, if possible, we left that rather dubious amenity for the ladies. Not that Myra ever availed herself of it—the long wooden seat was rough and mildew damp, she said, preferring to risk the occasional stinging nettle and cuch down behind the big old tombstone at the top of the graveyard whenever necessary. And judging by the muffled giggles and gasps which often reached the ears of the philosophically astride-stanced males at the church yard wall, she wasn't the only one!

I was just doing up my last button when I became aware of the unmistakable roar of Dai's motorbike and sidecar tearing up the hill. Where the hell had he been to till now, I wondered as I strolled round to the front of the hall in time to see Dai hastily dismounting.

He peered through the darkness. "Evan, boy! Am I glad to see you!" he gasped, taking off his goggles and giving his face a wipe. "There's a time I've had!" His voice sounded desperate.

"Where the hell have you been, then?" I pressed.

"Is Ann inside?" he worried, ignoring my question.

"Why aye, man, of course she is, and . . ." Dai caught hold of my arm, gave a quick, almost furtive look round and pulled me to the dark side of the hall.

"What the . . ."

"Listen boy," he whispered closely, "There's trouble I'm in now!" and he cursed resoundingly under his breath. "I had this message from Sybil, see, saying that if I knew what was good for me I'd go over to The Farmer's to see her tonight. So, of course, I had no choice." His face glistened in the gloom as I listened intently to his tale. "Determined, she is!" he lamented, wiping his face once more. "Says she'll accuse me in public—and she's got a string of dates, from God knows where, to prove her claim! What the hell am I going to do, man?" And he paced back and fore like a caged tiger.

"Buggered if I know," I said, unhelpfully.

Dai clutched at my arm again. "I mean, fair play, it wasn't my fault—I swear it wasn't me, Evan!"

I nodded my belief.

"You've got to think of something!" he demanded.

"Me?" Really taken aback I was. "There's nothing I can do, Dai," I reasoned.

"You're my last hope, man. I can't marry her, Evan, fair

111

play now!'' And I agreed that marrying Sybil from The Farmer's Arms was unthinkable, but what I could do to prevent such an occurrence was beyond me.

"I'll think of something, boy, don't you worry," I consoled, sounding far more confident than I felt.

Dai visibly relaxed. "There's a pal!" he breathed thankfully, giving me an appreciative slap on the back. "Have they had The Supper yet?" he went on, "I'm bloody famished—I'll tell Ann I had to go over to Harford about some slates," he suggested as we shoved open the Church Hall doors and entered the yellow-bright gaslit room, crowded with post-mortem holding, groups of whist players. Clouds of white dust were rising from the floor as The Vicar expertly scattered French chalk over the splintery planks in an attempt to give them a bit of slide ready for the dancing and Old Jenkins blew a sharp blast on his whistle and announced that The Supper was now ready.

Dai gave his trousers a quick dust down and wiped the toes of his shoes against the back of his legs as a smiling Myra and Ann came over to us to be led into The Supper Room. Mr. Tyler took Ruby firmly by the arm and guided her to a pair of seats near the ham, Captain and Mrs. Rees-Williams took their customary places at the top of the table and The Vicar and his wife sat themselves down at the bottom while we four found four chairs somewhere in the unimportant middle. And as I sat myself down I realised, too late, that I had picked a place right by a set of unaccommodating trestles.

But there's a grand feast we tucked into—thick slices of cold ham, fluffy boiled potatoes and spicy pickles, followed by Myra's trifles and Welshcakes and as many cups of strong tea as we wanted. Fit for The King himself it was, and Mrs. Rees-Williams's floral arrangements looked a treat and we all made sure we told her so. Habit it was, that's all, mind.

No sooner was the last Welshcake washed down by the last drop of well-stewed tea than up jumped Miss Gwendoline Davies, all of a fluster, to go and wind up the gramophone and within minutes the foot-tapping music came echoing in from the empty hall. Miss Davies was always in charge of the gramophone, seeing as she was the musical member of the community. Immediately there was a rush for all the ladies to change into their dancing shoes, the Supper helpers whipped off their pinnies and the daring ones powdered their faces and coloured their lips in the privacy of the corner behind the tea urns. And Umshla surreptitiously tiptoed out through the back door and made his way home.

Jenkins the Schoolmaster announced The St. Bernard's and fifty pairs of Llanporth feet sent the French chalk flying as they waltzed and stamped around the dusty-white hall. One-steps and Valetas, Two-steps and Waltzes, Gay Gordons and tangos followed perspiringly one after another, with Old Jenkins roaring "Grand Chain!" as a reminder to the swirling breathless dancers as The Lancers got under way. Anybody could see he loved being a Schoolmaster the way he undertook his duties as M.C. Really ordered us about he did!

We had barely recovered from the hectic pace of The Lancers when Miss Davies was furiously winding up the gramophone for The Grand March. Faces flushed and glistening, we all heaved ourselves up from the chairs we had so recently collapsed into. Jenkins positioned himself at the top of the hall, the music blared forth and down the middle of the hall we all paraded in single file, swinging our arms like soldiers, marching up to Old Jenkins who parted us 'Ladies to the Right, Gents to the Left'. Round we marched until we met up in pairs at the bottom of the hall, then up to Jenkins we marched arm in arm to be parted in pairs to the left and right again—then in fours, then eights, then sixteens, until there was so much hilarious stamping and laughing that you couldn't hear Miss Davies's gramophone at all! And by the time the final join up came and every one of the dancers hecticly endeavoured to march in one long link-armed line up the too narrow hall, everything collapsed into hilarious chaos as it always did.

Jenkins had to blow his whistle three times before anybody took any notice, and we all tried to pull ourselves together into a respectful frame of mind as Captain Rees-Williams stood to attention and started to sing God Save The King. Unfortunately we didn't possess a record of The National Anthem for Miss Davies to put on, so it was always a bit of a straggly start, but, by damn, we made sure we gave it a good finish in full resounding four part harmony.

The air was cool and fresh as Myra and I made our way down the hill with our laundry basket. We had been almost the last to leave the hall as we'd had to wash up the trifle basins before stacking them into the basket once more. Our footsteps echoed through the deserted High Street as we passed each curtain darkened window, swinging our laundry basket between us.

"Those cockles must be doing you good, Evan," Myra suddenly remarked.

I tripped awkwardly over a loose paving stone as my co-ordination faltered. "What makes you say that, then?"

"Well, you didn't catch a cold after all, did you?"

"No," I laughed, "By damn, I didn't!"

We continued for a while in silence.

"The trifles were nice."

"Lovely," I agreed, "and the Welshcakes."

"Pity Mrs. L. Y. T. Jones missed the First Prize though— Jenkins the Schoolmaster's wife is always getting it."

"Mh," I agreed, wincing at the memory of the withering look Mrs. L. Y. T. Jones had bestowed on me when it was announced that she'd lost by only one point.

We had just put the basket down to change sides and were setting off once more when we both became aware of a murmur of voices coming from a huddle of shadows in the gloom ahead of us.

"What's that down by there, then?" Myra wondered. I peered ahead as the official voice of P.C. Llewellyn reached our ears.

"On your feet now, come on. On your feet!" he ordered a far-gone Dago, lying paralytic on the pavement. Dull Reggie plucked ineffectively at the loose coat wrapped round the snoring bundle as P.C. Llewellyn continued to remonstrate. They both looked up at our approach.

"Where's Mrs. Dago Jones and the pram tonight, then?" I asked, surprised at her non-appearance.

"Blowed if I know . . . can't understand it." P.C. Llewellyn pushed back his helmet and scratched his head. "But he can't stay by 'ere all night," he stated flatly, thwacking his wooden spoon booby prize with great authority against his side. "Dull Reggie here can't shift him on his own see, so I'll just have to put him in my cell for the night."

"Aw, fair play now, you don't want to go and do that," I argued, feeling a certain amount of loyalty to Mrs. Dago

Jones. I looked down at the snoring crumpled figure at my feet. "I'll tell you what . . . Myra and I'll just pop home with the trifle dishes and I'll bring the basket back. Dull Reggie and me can carry him home in it, no trouble."

Myra looked over at me in surprise.

"How does that suit you?" I asked P.C. Llewellyn. He continued to thwack his wooden spoon thoughtfully, obviously loathe to miss the opportunity of having something worthwhile to enter in his Duty Book.

"Oh, all right then," he eventually conceded, no doubt realising all the bother he could save himself.

I was back within five minutes to find him trying, without much success, to carry on a conversation with Dull Reggie while old Dago Jones continued to sleep blissfully and noisily at their feet.

"In with him then, boys!" I ordered, and the uncomplaining bundle was unceremoniously dumped into Myra's washing basket, his head lolling over one side while his legs hung limply over the other. Dull Reggie pointed a fat finger at the slumped Dago and gave an appreciative chuckle before bending to pick up the handle on my count of one, two, three, up.

"Light as a feather he is," I assured a dubious looking P.C. Llewellyn. "We'll have him home in no time. Won't we Reggie?" And Reggie grinned gormlessly as he nodded his heavy head.

"Well, I'm obliged to you, Mr. Evans," thanked the Llanporth Arm of The Law, touching his helmet officially with his wooden spoon as we marched off up the hill with our sozzled cargo.

I knew it would be a waste of time trying to converse with my fellow helper, so knowing his appreciation of a bit of good music, I started up with Mochyn Du. And by the time we'd reached The Pump at the Top End, Reggie's voice was exploring the registers of three octaves with joyful abandon and complete disregard of either time or tune.

The dimly outlined pair of cottages cut across the skyline as we rounded the last bend to the accompaniment of the fifth chorus of Mochyn Du. A single light shone sparingly across the unkempt front gardens and the plaintive cries of two babies mingled discordantly from within. We crunched our way across the noisy cockle shells.

"Sh!" I cautioned a still warbling Reggie.

"Sh!" He repeated, putting a thick finger to his lips and giving a slack mouthed grin.

As we put our laden basket carefully down on the ground I caught a glimpse of Dago's usual chariot still standing under a makeshift tarpaulin lean-to, straggling against the cottage wall. Strange that, I thought as I made my way past the dark little window to the front door. Dago's missus had never been known to fail him before, come rain or snow.

I raised my hand to give a tap. Dago's snores continued their deep rhythmic rumble behind me and the next door's babies' cries grated plaintively on the night air.

The dark cottage remained undisturbed in spite of my rousing tap and I was just debating whether to try the latch when a stream of pale light cut across the next door wilderness as Mrs. Williams's front door opened and a straggle haired Mrs. Dago Jones, a grisling one year old over her shoulder, stood framed in the lamp light. She looked old and weary.

I turned and opened my mouth to explain my presence but she ignored me and walked over to Dull Reggie.

"Your Mam's just got a new little babby, Reggie . . . another little sister you've got." The baby on her shoulder opened its mouth wider and its cries rose to a screaming crescendo of complaint at being taken out into the cold night air while a feeble new-born wail filtered out with the hot foetid air from the open doorway.

Reggie patted the screaming baby's damp behind gently.

"No, no," explained Mrs. Dago Jones, "inside, she is . . . by your Mam."

His eyes slowly followed her pointing finger and in to the teeming little cottage he wandered.

"Another girl it is, then?" I asked, a little awkwardly.

Mrs. Dago Jones hitched the crying baby onto another shoulder and gave him a few ineffective, placating pats. She took a few steps towards Myra's laundry basket.

"There's good of you, Evan Evans," she slushed as she looked down at her blissfully snoring husband.

"I'll just carry him indoors and I'll be off then," I

volunteered, lifting the limp figure with some difficulty and edging my way in through the narrow doorway.

"He loves his Saturday nights," she confided juicily as I dumped him in his fireside chair. "Not that he remembers any of them, mind!" she added with a chuckle, sounding more like her usual self. The baby's complaining cries dwindled away to a rhythmic sucking as a comforting thumb found its way into its hungry, wet mouth. Mrs. Dago Jones reached behind the door and something soft and furry was pressed into my hand.

"Tell your Myra to make you a nice rabbit pie, Evan Evans!" she instructed, "A lovely change it will make from all those damn cockles!" And her chuckle followed me out into the clean night air. I slung Myra's washing basket over my back, coracle fashion, and down in the village the Church clock struck one.

Good God, I thought, it's Sunday. And as my footsteps echoed down the hill the old rhyme lilted through my head . . .

> Monday's child is fair of face,
> Tuesday's child is full of grace,
> Wednesday's child is full of woe,
> Thursday's child has far to go,
> Friday's child works hard for a living,
> Saturday's child is loving and giving,
> But the child that's born on the Sabbath Day
> Is blythe and bonny, and good and gay.

I took a last backward look at the pale light struggling through the Williams's grimy laced window . . . blythe and bonny, and good and gay . . . well, perhaps she would be . . . perhaps, poor dab.

Chapter 8

The disturbed attic dust tickled my nostrils into an explosive sneeze as I searched the piles of long forgotten books for my old Latin primer. I'd remembered seeing it somewhere when I'd come up looking for my whip and top and it was that which had given me an idea as to how to solve Dai's rather pressing problem.

The mouth-watering, savoury aroma of the Sunday Roast Beef filtered up through the trap door as I continued with my dusty search. Myra had put the beef and the rice pudding in the oven before setting out for chapel, but I'd excused myself from accompanying her on the pretext of having a pressing amount of book-keeping to do for the shop, so she'd gone leaving me strict instruction to turn the roast potatoes over at a quarter to twelve.

My mind had been too active for sleep when I'd eventually reached home the previous night with my empty laundry basket and my poached rabbit and I'd lain in the deep warm hollow of our soft feather bed and turned Dai's problem over in my mind. Gradually a brilliant plan of campaign had come to me and my old Grammar School Latin Primer and Pa's old travelling leather desk were two of the key instruments in its successful execution.

Aha! I thought with satisfaction as the elusive textbook finally revealed itself in the flickering candlelight. I placed the once hated Latin Primer by the edge of the trap door and cautiously made my way over the joists to the other side of the attic for the next essential piece of equipment.

The once lovingly polished leather was dulled with a thick layer of dust. It must have been at least twenty years since Pa had put his treasured desk up there. I picked up the surprisingly heavy leather case, made my way back across the joists, tucked my Latin Primer under my arm, blew out the candle and climbed back down through the trap door onto the top of the chest of drawers which had always stood conveniently on the landing beneath. Carefully I slid the trap door over the opening, jumped down from the chest of drawers and made my way excitedly down the stairs to the kitchen with my trophies.

A plain piece of suitably age-yellowed paper, cut with my

razor from one of Pa's big old account books, lay spread out on the table in readiness. I put the dust laden travelling desk on the sideboard and sat down at the table with my Latin Primer with keen anticipation. I flicked through a few pages, catching glimpses of unlearnable vocabularies and incomprehensible declensions in my search for the most impressive Latin-like piece of Latin prose I could find.

Memories of sitting at ink-stained, initial-scarred desks vainly grappling with unfathomable pieces of translation while Old Snapper Thompson's corncrake voice droned endlessly on about accusatives, vocatives, ablatives and genitives, future perfects and past participles, flowed vividly back. I shuddered at the memory.

Page 17 . . . now that looks an impressive bit, I thought and I unscrewed my fountain pen and copied a few experimental words onto a spare piece of paper in a fair imitation of Pa's old-fashioned copperplate handwriting . . .

Variat tamen memoria eius rei.

I viewed the effect with a critical eye. It didn't look right somehow . . . the ink . . . that was it . . . it was the wrong colour—and the nib was too thick. I gave a quick look at the clock. There was still a good hour before Myra would be home, I thought as I nipped into the darkened shop and ransacked the back of the till drawer for a bottle of indian ink and an old dip-in pen which had been there for donkey's years.

I sat down and tried again. The clock ticked quietly on and the fine steel nib scratched noisily across the paper as I concentrated on the thin up-strokes and the thick down strokes. I held my efforts at arms length with a satisfied smile on my face. Really great it looked. A few more minutes spent practising artistically decorative scrolls on the first letter R and, at last, I considered I was ready to begin the actual manuscript. I dipped the pen into the ink once more, poised it above the virgin paper, held my breath and started to write.

From vague recollections I gathered I was writing about some crazy idea to carry elephants across a river in order to do battle somewhere—Latin was always about some damn battle or other it seemed, I recalled ruefully as I paused at what appeared a judicious place to insert Dai's name . . .

More than twenty minutes had passed before I finished my document, and by damn, when I read it through I felt really proud of it.

Variat tamen memoria eius rei. Secundum nonnullos scriptores ratem longam a terra in Poeni flumen porrigunt; tum ean ad ripam religant et iam sililem pontis humo consternunt. Deinde ratis brevoir longiori vinculis copulatur. Sex tum elephanti una cum feminis per *David Alwyn Rees* stabilem ratem velut per viam incedunt; ubi ratem breviorem intraverunt, hominas £50 vincula resolvunt et ratem navigiis trahunt. Excidunt ob trepidationem aliquot £26 ex elephantis in flumen; nihilominus sine rectoribus, *Llanporth, 14th September 1925,* propter pondus suum stabiles, veda quaerunt et in terram evadunt.

I finished it off with a large indecipherable signature scrawled with a flourish at the bottom and sat back with a sigh of satisfaction. Really enjoyed myself, I had, it only remained for me to put two rows of dots underneath for further signatures and everything would be complete. My free hand attempts, on my spare piece of paper, to keep the dots tidily level, being non too successful, I searched, in vain, in the sideboard drawers for a ruler. Pa's travelling desk! There was sure to be one in there. I pulled out my handkerchief and started to wipe away the thickly layered dust.

Evan Curtis Evans—poor old Pa, I thought reminiscently as I stared at the gleaming lustre of the gold letters E.C.E. gradually being revealed by my handkerchief duster. The clock chiming the three-quarters broke in on my reverie, I gave myself a shake, flicked open the two catches, folded back the lid and opened out the side flaps.

The calfskin writing pad shone dully between the age old inkstains and the musty smell of long forgotten shop accounts rose to my nostrils. Two heavy cut-glass inkpots, their red and black contents long since dried up, stood stolidly at one side and two rusty nibbed pens lay in a shallow groove alongside a cylindrical ebony ruler. I picked up the foot length of polished black-dense wood and placed it in position on my Latin document. I drew my row of dots, rolled it down an inch and drew another row beneath.

Now for the next procedure. Conscious of the quickly passing time I dashed back into the shop and snipped a length of narrow pink ribbon from the roll, rushed out to the back kitchen for a candle and retrieved a stick of red sealing wax from the table drawer.

And with Pa's Latin-inscribed account-book page neatly rolled up I swiftly tied it up with the pink ribbon, melted the wax over the candle and let it drop in a large blob to seal down the edge of the paper, pressing an imprint of my signet ring into the wax before it hardened.

The clock was just striking twelve as I tucked the precious document into the leather travelling desk. Quickly I poured the Indian ink into one of the heavy glass bottles, replaced the ebony ruler along with my extra dip-in pen, folded the desk up and thankfully clicked the catches shut.

It took but a few minutes to clear everything away and to slip the travelling desk in the bottom of the back bedroom wardrobe alongside a paper bag containing Pa's old spats and bowler hat and his black tie and spectacles and my own brown leather gloves which Mam had given me the previous Christmas. Pa's leather collar box still stood on the chest of drawers and when I'd chosen one of his rounded stiff collars and placed it in the bag with the rest of my accoutrements, my preparations were finally complete.

*   *   *

The roast beef was delicious and the roast potatoes, even though I'd forgotten to turn them over, had been crackly crisp with fatty meat juices.

"More rice pudding?" Myra offered as I sat back replete and contented.

Tempting though it was, I managed to exert enough self control to refuse and said that I'd take a stroll over to Dai's instead to see about the arrangements for tomorrow's work up at Tŷ Mawr, hoping to catch him before he set off to show Ann the somewhat dubious mystical properties of the Bleeding Tree at Nevern.

"You've only got just enough cockles left for tea," reminded Myra as I stood before the mirror checking that there was no dinner left on my moustache and setting my Sunday trilby at the correct angle.

"Aw dast . . . I don't know how I'm going to find time to get some more. Busy, I'll be all day tomorrow." I stared at my reflection with a frown, wondering if I dare suggest going cockling on a Sunday.

"And you can't go cockling on a Sunday," Myra pointed out, reading my thoughts with uncanny accuracy.

"I'll think of something," I assured her as I turned to make my way through the passage. "I won't be long," I called back as I stepped out onto the pavement.

After the few days of squally wind and scudding rain clouds, the Indian Summer seemed to have temporarily returned and the High Street warmed itself in the autumn sun's rays as I straightened back my shoulders, pulled in my rather over-full Sunday stomach and strode purposefully down the deserted road. Deserted, that is, except for the aimlessly dawdling figure of Dull Reggie.

No wonder he spent so much of his time, day and night, wandering around the town, I thought, recalling how impossible it must be to find a spare inch to sit down in that cramped little cottage of theirs. How they'd find room for the latest addition I couldn't imagine.

"Hey, Reggie!" I called, crossing the road as an idea suddenly came into my head. "Tomorrow," I said very clearly, placing myself directly in front of him and staring him straight in the face so that my words might have more effect, "Tomorrow, you get me a bucket of cockles." And I fished in my pocket and held out a silver threepenny bit.

He put out his hand to take it.

"Tomorrow," I insisted clearly. "Cockles for me tomorrow . . . you come and get a bucket."

He looked at me through his thick, dark lashes and bent down to scratch his dirty bare knee thoughtfully.

"Cockles, tomorrow," he repeated.

"Good lad," I commended, giving him a smile.

"Got a new baby," he grinned, still scratching his knee.

"Yes, I know—well done, Reggie!" and I clapped him on the back of my old green pullover, the front of which was already liberally smeared with jam and gravy, and the sleeves encrusted from their mis-use as a handkerchief.

"After school, tomorrow then," I reminded as I left him aimlessly kicking at the tufts of grass growing between the paving stones. It would be a good job when he left school at Christmas so that he could wear long trousers, I thought to myself. A hulking great boy like that—made him look worse those short trousers did.

My hands turned a little clammy as I passed by Number 16's front door and wondered what Ruby and Matthew Tyler were doing at that moment. Myra had said that Ruby'd worn a new fox fur to Chapel that morning and she'd thought they'd made a lovely pair, him with his uniform of course. As bad as P.C. Llewellyn he was—always in uniform the pair of them. I reckon they were afraid to take it off in case they just looked like everybody else!

I was just wondering if he ever did take it off when my somewhat ribald imagery was interrupted by the sound of Dai's Royal Enfield rounding the bend at the bottom of the hill. I signalled him down and spent the next five minutes acquainting him with the details of my brilliant scheme for rescuing him from the marital clutches of the obliging barmaid at The Farmer's Arms. He listened intently, his eyes opening wider and wider in appreciative admiration of my undisputed ingenuity as the Enfield ticked over smoothly beneath him.

"Bloody marvellous! Bloody marvellous you are boy! Just made my day you have!" he grinned, his tanned face beaming with relief. "I'll go straight over to The Farmer's tomorrow dinnertime . . . straight over from Tŷ Mawr . . . and tell her exactly what you said." And he put a supercilious look on his face as he put on his best *crachach* accent and proclaimed, "I've put the entire affair in the hands of my solicitor who will be calling on you at eight o'clock this evening . . . prompt!"

And we both burst out laughing.

"See you, boy," he called as he flicked the bike into gear, opened the throttle and roared off up the hill to the Tugwell's to pick up his Ann, giving me a backward wave as I made my own way home to take Myra up on that second helping of rice pudding—well, fair play, it did have sultanas in it, and if there's one thing I can't resist, it's a juicy sultana.

*　　　　*　　　　*

Myra and I were rudely awakened before six the following morning by a persistent heavy hammering on the back kitchen door.

"Who the devil is that?" I grumbled, climbing reluctantly out of the warm bed and stumbling half asleep down the stairs. "It's hardly daylight!" I muttered evilly to myself as I drew back the bolts and peered with bleary eyes at the large figure standing outside.

Dull Reggie!

Aw hell! I thought in disbelief. Not now!

"Bucket!" he reminded me, holding out his hand.

With great restraint I managed to squash a suitable expletive which flashed unbidden through my head and instead started to explain, with admirable patience, that I had instructed him to call *after school* not at damn day-break. But half way through I looked at those blank, beautiful brown eyes and resignedly abandoned the idea.

"All right, Reggie," I agreed. "Come on," and I winced my barefoot way across the cold back yard to fetch a pail from the shed.

"Cockles now!" I cautioned, in case he got it into his head to bring back a load of mussels or winkles or anything else which took his fancy.

"Like these." and I picked up a handful of shells off the garden to show him exactly what I wanted. I wished him good luck, thrust my sawn off garden rake into his left hand, warned him not to be late for school and hobbled back across the yard clutching my pyjamas round me against the early morning chill.

I poured the water into the kettle with a shiver, set it on the oil stove and retreated to the comparative warmth of the rag mat in the kitchen. A nice surprise for Myra it would be to have a cup of tea brought up to her for a change, I thought. I wriggled my cold toes appreciatively through the thick rags and stared glumly at the dead fire in the grate.

I really ought to light the fire . . . I really ought. Reluctantly I knelt before the comfortless grey ashes, picked up the poker and resignedly started to rake the cinders. An old newspaper I found under the cushion of Pa's old windsor chair and in seconds it was screwed up and placed on the clean ash-raked cinders and covered with an artistically arranged criss-cross of sticks that Myra had judiciously left in the fender. A shovel of coal from the scuttle, a match, and soon the warming glow of the licking flames and the sound of the kettle beginning to sing out in the back kitchen, made my spirits start to rise.

A lovely surprise it would be, I thought once more as I carefully carried the steaming cups up the stairs—and we'd have a nice hour to while away before getting up, I speculated with pleasurable anticipation. And I don't mind telling you it wasn't an extra hours kip I was contemplating neither! Good job Reggie was getting me a fresh supply of cockles!

*　　　　*　　　　*

The sun was up and the morning well aired by the time I set out for Dai's yard over three hours later.

Front doorsteps were already being washed, pavements brushed and The Pump, with its attendant gossipers, was in full swing. Perry the Milk was leaping off and on his springy gig with his customary agility and ladling out his gills, pints and quarts into the waiting jugs at each door with the unerring accuracy of long practice, Mick The Prince was supervising the delivery of a dozen barrels into his cellar with a wary eye and Cy Lloyd the Butcher was sprinkling Dai's sawdust over the shop floor in readiness for the day's customers.

A hive of industry it was on a Monday morning in Llanporth, I can tell you, and as I turned into Dai's yard, swinging Pa's leather travelling desk in one hand and clutching my paper bag in the other, I was well pleased to be a part of it.

"Magnificent, it is," breathed Dai as he viewed the sealing waxed and pink ribboned scroll.

"What's it say inside?"

"Buggered if I know," I grinned, "Something about a battle and a load of elephants crossing a river—I think!"

We stood in The Coffin Shed inspecting the various contents of the paper bag. "Where's your Pa's funeral suit, then?" I asked.

"Over by there—I hope it fits." Dai looked critically at the long frock coat and black pinstripe trousers hanging behind the ledged and braced door.

I tried on the coat and the sharp strong smell of camphor hung on the air around me.

"Fits like a glove—that's a bit of luck, isn't it? I won't bother trying on the trousers now this minute." I held the pinstripes up against me. "They look as if they'll be all right. I'll come over at half past seven tonight then and we'll get ready for the 'attack'!" Taking my tone from my Latin scroll!

As I shrugged off Old Mr. Rees's frock coat my eyes scanned the wood cluttered shed.

"Where's my Tabitha then?" surely she wasn't still over at Glynmawr I thought.

"Well, boy . . ." and Dai inhaled deeply on his newly lit Woodbine, . . . "I expect you noticed Umshla Watkins coming over to have a chat with me after The Supper on Saturday Night . . . just before he went home because the Dancing was starting it was."

I nodded, puzzled as to what it had to do with Tabitha.

"Well, you'll never guess what he wanted, boy!"

I waited, mystified.

"Wanted to know if he could hire your Tabitha for a couple of evenings a week for a bit of personal First Aid practice!"

I opened my eyes wide in disbelief.

"A fact, man," Dai assured me, expertly flicking his ash into the spare coffin—very particular about ash on the floor he was—well, a fire hazard it would be with all those shavings about. "Mind you, he said he couldn't afford two bob a night—offered me sixpence, so we shook hands on it! Came along late after Chapel last night and carried her home—wrapped up, of course—along the back lane. Well, it's only three doors away after all."

A grin spread slowly across my face as light suddenly dawned.

"His Mam's away down in Pontypridd!" I announced with a wink., We both stared at each other, reading each other's mind and we both roared with laughter.

"I bet you ten bob it isn't First Aid he's practising!" Dai managed to gasp.

"You never know boy—he's a bit straight laced after all," I reasoned, recalling the look of stunned embarrassment on his face when he'd peered into Frank's guardsvan. "When's he bringing her back then?"

"Late tonight—he knows the door's always open."

"Well, I'll be . . ." and I shook my head at the unexpected

turn of events as I stacked Pa's travelling desk and my paper bag of accoutrements into the spare coffin and went out to help a still chuckling Dai to lift a bag of cement into the sidecar, along with a bucket of lime and a sack of sand.

Dai lowered his goggles into place. ''All set?''

I gripped the pillion with my knees and placed my hands on Dai's hips. ''All set!'' I called back. The Enfield answered obediently to the kick and out of the yard we roared.

Lovely it was, racing through the air along the Front Road. The estuary sparkled in the early sun and the mudflats gleamed a silver ribbon alongside the ebb tide. I narrowed my eyes against the rushing air and turned my face to one side, vowing as I did each time I rode pillion, to buy myself a pair of goggles before the next time. The bike purred powerfully beneath us and our overalls flapped madly in the rushing wind as we sped along.

There was no sign of Dull Reggie on the water's edge, I noticed. Perhaps he'd gone back by now, I was thinking, when my speeding gaze happened to fall on a lone bent figure crouched over a bucket, up on the dry shingle by the sea wall. It was Dull Reggie all right.

''Stop the bike!'' I yelled in Dai's ear, pointing down to the figure on the beach just ahead of us.

Dai throttled back and brought us to a swerving halt by the sea wall.

''Won't be a minute,'' I explained, ''Just want to see how many cockles Dull Reggie's got for me—and to make sure he remembers to go to bloody school!''

I jumped down onto the loose shingle, calling and waving my hand. Reggie looked up and beamed in recognition.

''How's it going then, Reggie? 'I greeted, noticing with some surprise, how commendably clean he'd managed to keep himself.

''Cockles!'' He assured me with a few slow nods and bent down to continue his task.

My smile of congratulation faded on my lips, however, as I watched him painstakingly pick up the empty dry cockle shells and place them carefully in the almost full bucket.

I peered in without hope. Now I knew the reason why there was no mud on his boots—the bucket was filled with cockleshells all right—empty half shells without a single living creature in any of them!

Aw, hell! I thought for the second time that morning on encountering his unpredictable behaviour and limited comprehension. Sadly I shook my head—it was all my fault, I realised, as I watched him continue his careful search through the barren dry shingle—I shouldn't have shown him those damn empty shells in the back garden!

Gently I caught hold of his shoulder and lifted him up. "No, no, Reggie," I explained patiently, "Big, fat cockles I want." I cupped my hands in the rough shape of a live cockle. "Like this." I bent and picked up two halves and joined them together. "See?"

He studied them intently, his brow furrowed with concentration.

"Fat cockles." he repeated earnestly. Suddenly his dirty face broke into a grin. "Fat cockles, fat cockles!" he chuckled, the phrase momentarily tickling his artless sense of humour.

"Down by there," I motioned, directing his vacant gaze toward the ebb tide mudflats. He grinned and nodded.

Reluctantly I tipped the bucketful of empty shells out onto the shingle, conscious of Reggie's eyes watching my action. I rose, expecting a look of disappointment on his face, but he was still bloody smiling! Happily he picked up the rake and the empty bucket, the precious hours of painstaking shell collecting already forgotten as he trudged purposefully towards the edge of the tide. I opened my mouth to recall him, realising that there was no time left now as he should be on his way to school, but, what the hell, I thought, he may as well occupy himself picking cockles as struggle with the indecipherable complexities of reading with Ann Thomas. And, besides, I'd suddenly remembered that the tide would be too high for cockling when he came out at four o'clock!

Dai's horn brought me hurrying back up to The Front. I gave a last look at Reggie's retreating back as he plodded his way down through the mud. With a bit of luck I'd have a pail full of cockles waiting for me by the time I arrived home that afternoon, I thought, as we roared off once more towards Tŷ Mawr, and I decided, magnanimously, that I'd give Reggie an extra penny for the original misunderstanding regarding the desirability of gathering cockle shells with, if possible, actual cockles inside them!

But, there's a dull cuckoo he was, fair play!

Chapter 9

Tŷ Mawr stood imposingly three gabled behind high grey stone walls, its intricate wrought iron gates, flanked with heavy ball-capitolled pillars, opening up a vista of smooth green lawns on either side of a wide gravel drive. I caught a fleeting glimpse of Captain Rees-Williams's De Dion Bouton gleamingly parked outside the front door as Dai drove straight past and pulled us in at the narrower gateway of the Tradesmen's Entrance twenty yards further along the narrow winding road.

As the Enfield's roar subsided the raucous caw of the rooks in the high surrounding trees and the shriek of the ever hungry seagulls echoed on the air. It was a sheltered spot with the tall headland of Mawr Point diverting the ever present westerlies around the secluded haven. The side gate gave a complaining creak as I pushed it open for Dai to stagger through with his bag of cement. An untidy pile of a hundred or so old quay stones lay tipped to one side and Dai's wheelbarrow lay upside down on top.

"Where've we got to take them to then?" I asked, seeing no obvious break in the stone walling skirting the road.

"Over by there," he pointed, "Round the back and down by the beach. Lovely and easy it would have been if we hadn't gone and sunk old Tut-Tut's bloody boat," he added ruefully. "We'll take the cement and sand down first," he suggested, heaving the heavy bags onto the barrow and throwing his crowbar and trowels in alongside, "Then you can keep fetching the stones while I get on with the repair—all right?" I picked up the bucket of lime and nodded, the arrangement suiting me fine.

The morning sun beamed warmly on our backs as we made our way down the path, past the kitchen door and along the edge of the back lawn to the lower boundary wall, it was a bit of a devious route, but, as Dai pointed out, we couldn't go bee-lining across the grass, really churn it up that loaded barrow would.

"Let's have a fag before we start then," I took the proferred Woodbine gratefully and struck a match on the tumble-down stone wall behind us. A brightly chintzed, swinging garden seat stood alongside a white wrought-iron table in the centre of the lawn, but thinking it might be a little presumptious on our part to take advantage of it, we flung ourselves down on the grass instead and leant back on the warm stones as we puffed appreciatively on our fags.

"Bloody magnificent house, mind, Evan," commented Dai reverently, viewing Tŷ Mawr with screwed up eyes through a blue smoke haze. "Just look at those decorated bargeboards— and those lovely finials—a beautiful bit of carving that is. And fancy having voussoirs round the back as well as at the front—perfectly cut they are too." he added, respectfully, obviously impressed by the high standard of workmanship.

I wasn't quite sure where to look in order to appreciate these undoubted architectural refinements, but agreed, nevertheless, that it was truly a bloody magnificent house.

"And only three buggers live in it! Two when that Selina goes back to college." He sighed, regretfully.

"Aye," I agreed, thinking of Dull Reggie's teeming little cottage.

There was a sudden gush of water into the drain beneath the kitchen window—there's lovely it must be to have drains, I thought enviously—the back door opened and out came Mrs. Nellie Williams's eldest girl who worked as the daily maid. She shook a bright yellow duster half heartedly.

"She's quite a nice little thing," judged Dai grudgingly, his mind quickly abandoning the appreciation of beautiful finials and well-cut voussoirs for the contemplation of the more comely embellishments of Mrs. Nellie Williams's eldest.

"Not half as nice as that up by there, boy!" I countered, sucking in a quick breath of admiration.

Dai followed my eye up to the upstairs wooden balcony where young Selina, beautiful luscious young Selina, stood draped in some sort of flowing, pale orange, satin robe, stretching herself in the warm sunshine.

Dai gave a deep appreciative growl in his throat, then quickly jumped up, flicked his fag end over the wall, gave himself a determined shake and suggested with a regretful sigh that she was out of our class and we'd better get on with mending her bloody wall.

"By the way, Dai," I asked, off-hand, as I bent to lift the handles of the empty wheelbarrow, "Do you like cockles?"

"Can't stand 'em, boy!" he retorted, and my spirits sank to my boots as Mrs. Dago Jones's theory lessened in validity, for after all, there was no-one randier than Dai, now was there?

"Had so much of the damn things when I was a kid," he grunted, crowbarring the loose stones away, "it put me right off 'em!" And my spirits lifted once more—my faith restored.

Bloody ironic it was though, I thought ruefully as I set off up the path for my first load of stones, that all the blessed time I was swallowing her evil-smelling preventative concoctions, there was Dai's Mam filling him up with mountains of damn cockles! No wonder we grew up with different degrees of . . . well, of . . . no wonder we grew up differently, that's all! But I was well on my way to redressing the balance, I assured myself cheerfully.

"Mix another banker, Evan, before you go back for another load, there's a pal," Dai asked as I returned with my barrow of stones. "Three to one and a bit of lime—and fill the bucket with some more water from that stand tap over by the garage will you?"

I bent to pick up the shovel.

"Hey boy," and Dai nudged me in the ribs. "Do you think that's for us, then?"

I looked up and there walking mincingly across the lawn was Mrs. Nellie Williams's eldest, now sporting a frilly white apron and carrying an enormous tray laden with what looked like a tall, silver tea-pot with a matching milkjug and sugar basin and two delicately patterned china cups and saucers. Carefully she made her way over to the wrought iron table and placed the tray and its expensively elegant contents on it.

We waited hopefully for a signal instructing us to go and help ourselves, but there was none forthcoming. Instead, out of the French windows stepped a smiling Selina accompanied by the weed of a boyfriend we'd seen her with at the Dance the previous Saturday.

"What the hell has she got on?" muttered Dai, his eyes popping, his compo-filled trowel halted in mid air.

The loosely belted oyster satin robe glinted and gleamed with each undulation as Selina gracefully strolled across the lawn. I racked my brains for the right word—Cardiff Hughes had shown me one the last time I'd called, but I'd thought it a bit too fancy for anyone in Llanporth to buy—I mean, Myra had a lovely nice warm dressing gown—blue it was, but it didn't look anything like this fabulous creation. Mind you, that satin couldn't have been very warm, and that was what I always thought dressing gowns were supposed to do—keep you warm. And fancy wearing it out in the garden! And at eleven o'clock in the morning too! There'd be some funny looks if the ladies of Llanporth, no matter what League they were in, suddenly started wandering down to The Pump for a can of water dressed like that, I can tell you. Why no, the only time a Llanporth dressing gown ever stepped outside a house was perhaps on the occasion of a furtive midnight dash down to the Tŷ Bach at the bottom of the garden—and then it would have to be a real emergency.

"Kimono!" I announced suddenly as the elusive word flashed into my head. Dai looked puzzled.

"A kimono—that's what that thing's called—a sort of fancy dressing gown," I explained.

Selina turned.

"There's a bloody great dragon on the back!" breathed Dai in disbelief. "Look, man!"

I caught a glimpse of a vividly green scrolled creature before Selina sat down, sending the garden seat swinging leisurely to and fro.

"Pour the coffee, Gerald darling." Her slightly bored voice carried clearly over the lawn as she elegantly flicked a lighter and lit a cigarette poised at the end of a six inch long holder.

Darling Gerald, clad in his immaculate white flannels and striped college blazer, did as he was bid without a murmur.

"Bloody fairy!" commented Dai scathingly. "I'd like to see him trying to re-build this bloody wall!" and he slapped the trowel of compo expertly into place.

We worked solidly for the next ten minutes—well, we did have an audience after all—while the delicate clatter of cups and the desultory chat filtered across the lawn.

"What they talking?" puzzled Dai in a whisper. "It's not Welsh is it?"

"Why no, boy—I think it must be French," I answered knowledgeably. "She's been to France this summer, you know—for nearly two months—so it said in The Telegraph."

"Look up, boy!" hissed Dai, as he carefully bedded down a hefty stone, "She's coming over by 'ere!"

"Ah . . . Mr. . . . um . . . Mr. . . . Rees, isn't it?" Dai looked up as if taken by surprise. "My friend," and Selina waved an arm vaguely in the direction of Darling Gerald, "has to catch the 11.45 train to Cardiff and Mummy and Daddy have taken the De Dion to a Rotary meeting at Carmarthen—Mummy's doing some shopping of course," she paused for breath and drew on her six inch cigarette holder, blowing the smoke down her nostrils like a steam engine. "I was wondering if you could possible give him a ride to the station in your . . . er . . . on your . . . motor cycle combination?" Terribly *crachach* her voice was.

"Why aye," agreed Dai, sounding even more broadly Pembrokeshire than usual by contrast, "if he doesn't mind a bit of cement dust on his trousers."

She smiled. "Ten minutes then?" and off she sauntered back to her swinging seat, leaving Dai and me hypnotised as we watched the scrolling green dragon rampantly flexing its claws across her deliciously undulating little bum.

Dai cleared his throat noisily and I took a deep breath. "Back to work, boy!" I reminded him with an effort.

"I'll tell you what," I suggested after a few minutes, "I'll carry on with the wall when you're gone, or all this damn compo will go off by the time you get back."

"Right you are, boy—and I may as well carry on over to The Farmers' Arms while I'm about it and inform that Sybil of your intended visit tonight." And he gave me a wink and an appreciative slap on the back before going to give the Enfield a bit of a dusting down. And I followed with the empty barrow.

Darling Gerald's matching leather suitcases were soon tucked safely into the sidecar and Dai sat astride the tank waiting for his passenger who was wrinkling his pointed nose in some distaste before gingerly cocking his leg over the pillion seat.

"Better hold on, boy!" shouted Dai as he revved up the engine threateningly.

Selina shrieked with amusement. "C'est très drôle, n'est ce pas, mon cheri?" she laughed.

Darling Gerald smiled weakly and reluctantly placed his hands on Dai's overall hips. Dai let out the clutch with a jolt, Selina called "Au revoir!" and Darling Gerald managed a brief half wave before hanging on grimly for dear life as the bike roared off up the drive, heeled through the gates and disappeared along the twisting, narrow road.

"Your friend's most obliging, Mr. . . . er . . . Mr. . . ."

"Mr. Evans, Evan Evans," I volunteered, blushing a bit, I felt sure, as my mind was full of oyster satin and green dragons and I didn't know quite where to look.

She smiled graciously, turned, and she and her dragon both disappeared inside the heavy oak front door. It closed with a resounding thud. Pity I wasn't Dressed for Drapery, I thought ruefully. A much better impression I would have made than in these scruffy old overalls—second hand they were at that—Dai had handed them on to me when he'd bought an extra pair last year. Ah well, I thought philosophically, as I loaded the barrow with three heavy stones and set off back, that's the way it goes.

"Finished for the day, then?" I asked in surprise, my barrow narrowly avoiding a head on collision with Mrs. Nellie Williams's eldest as she cycled round the corner of the house.

"Why no, Mr. Evans," she smirked, "Not till seven. Just got to pop down to Lewis the Grocer's with a list for Miss Selina, that's all." And off she wobbled up the path and out through the gate.

Quarter of an hour later I stood back from the wall and viewed my handiwork with a critical eye, comparing my five newly laid stones with Dai's expert workmanship. Not bad . . . not at all bad for a Draper, I thought complacently as I picked up the empty barrow and started to wheel it up the path for another load.

As I neared the kitchen a peculiar low whistling caught my attention. Somewhat puzzled, I quietly put down the barrow and peered in through the kitchen window.

It wasn't a kettle, for the fire range was bare and the gas cooker wasn't lit. The noise suddenly stopped, and just as I was about to move away, it just as suddenly started up again. Perhaps it was something that needed attention, I pondered. Cautiously I opened the kitchen door, automatically wiping my feet as I took a few hesitant steps inside.

By damn, it was bigger than our back kitchen, back room and parlour all put together, I marvelled, as my eyes searched for the source of the intermittent whistling. The long table lay bleach-scrubbed clean and the freshly blackened range reflected the banked up, flickering fire in its gleaming polish. My listening ears guided me over to the crockery laden Welsh dresser on the far wall, the noise appeared to be coming from a brass tube-like contraption fixed to the wall alongside the dresser. A short chain held a bung in place at the top.

Of course! A speaking tube! I knew they had them on board ships, and this must be one of Captain Rees-Williams's nautical innovations, for it was well known that he ran his household as if he were still on the bridge.

Cautiously I lifted the bung and was pleasantly rewarded with an instant cessation of the piercing whistle. I bent my ear to the tube somewhat nervously I must confess, and was astonished to hear a distorted voice calling my name!

"Mr. Evans! Mr. Evans, is that you?"

I blinked a few times in surprise, cleared my throat to give myself a few seconds to pull myself together and feebly answered "Yes."

"Mr. Evans, is that you?" the imperious voice repeated rather impatiently, obviously not having heard my reply. The reason was suddenly clear—I still had the damn tube by my ear instead of by my mouth! Quickly I remedied the situation and shouted "Yes" down the hole, fumbling frantically to get my ear in position quickly enough to catch what was being said next.

"There's no need to shout, Mr. Evans," came the reproof. I smiled apologetically. "Now, Mr. Evans, the bath plunger appears to have become stuck and I would be most obliged if you would come up and release it."

Bath plunger, I thought with some dismay, what the hell's a bath plunger? But I nodded anyway, willing to have a go, seeing as Dai wasn't available.

"Mr. Evans?"

Swiftly I made the necessary tube adjustment and stammered "Oh . . . er . . . yes Miss Rees Williams, I'll go up right this minute . . . er . . . where is the bathroom?"

"Up the stairs and the third door on the left—it's marked BATHROOM—you can't miss it . . . I think Daddy keeps some tools in the kitchen table drawer."

The tube went silent. I waited for a few seconds just to make sure there was nothing else, then carefully replaced the bung.

"Table drawer, table drawer," I muttered, walking round the vast scrubbed table pulling open various drawers until I found one containing an assortment of tools. I selected a hammer and a shifting spanner as the best possible implements and made my way over to the green baize door at the other side of the dresser.

It led directly into the dining room, a heavily mahoganied room dominated by a long, highly polished table surrounded by eight, tall, splat-backed chairs. Three gimlet eyed portraits of Captain Rees-Williams in various Nautical uniforms looked down from the walls and an enormous painting of a clipper ship in full sail hung over the fireplace.

Two rows of medals lay arrayed in a glass case on the silver candelabrad sideboard and a thick, richly patterned carpet absorbed my footfalls as I crossed to the opposite doorway, the silence broken only by the quiet ticking of the heavily brassed ship's clock hanging beside the clipper ship.

I stepped out into the hall. The heavy, slow tick of an enamelled faced grandfather's clock, standing on guard at the bottom of the stairs, took over from the quiet tick of the ship's clock as I left the dining room behind. I looked up. The sun streamed colourfully in through a large stained glass window reaching up to the landing. I caught hold of the smoothly polished mahogany handrail, took a deep breath, took a reassuring look at my hammer and shifting spanner and slowly started to climb.

BATHROOM. There it was in gold painted letters on the third door on the left. I hesitated a moment, gave a cautious little knock, just to be polite, although obviously there would be no-one inside, gripped the fluted brass door knob, pushed open the door and came face to face with the wicked red eyes of a rampant green dragon as Miss Selina Rees-Williams bent over the filled bath apparently wrestling with what must be The Plunger!

My mind froze, my mouth opened and closed like a damn fish, my hands gripped convulsively on my hammer and shifting spanner and my feet remained rooted to the spot. The oyster satin clung wetly to her newly bathed skin and in the same instant, my mind registered that even the lav seat, complete with lid, was made of polished mahogany.

Selina straightened up, turned and gave a slow, unmistakably welcoming smile. I tell you, if it hadn't been for those cockles I'd have stammered a panic-stricken apology and backed out in double quick time, but fortified by the fruits of the sea I threw down my hammer and spanner, strode across the steamy room—bigger than our shop it was—picked her up bodily, there's no other word for it, and followed her scarlet-nailed directing finger out onto the landing and in through a half open door at the far end.

We floated in on a cloud of unknown, indefinable perfume, I'll swear it wasn't California Poppy, Lily of the Valley nor that special stuff in the dark blue bottle I bought Myra for Christmas last year. But whatever it was, it was heady—very heady.

No fear of getting any splinters here, boy, I thought, staggering slightly under my load as I crossed the thick Indian carpet—I recognised it as Indian because I'd seen one in Cardiff Hughes's Emporium—and over to the eau-de-nil, silk covered double bed.

Modern interior sprung, not feather, I noted automatically as Selina bounced gently as I deposited her onto its silky softness.

By damn, I marvelled, as I joined her, this is the first time I've been in such intimate proximity with someone who's actually taken her C.W.B., let alone matriculated and got her Higher to boot, and the knowledge gave an added piquancy to the situation. And confidently fortified by the now undeniable aphrodisiacal qualities of the Welsh Cockle, I silently vowed, I'll give you Bell Tinko, my girl!

What the devil she was continuously whispering in my ear I had no idea, but just as my subconcious came to the conclusion that, of course, it was French, a sharp whistle nearly made me jump out of my skin. Well, fair play, that's all there was to jump out of at the time.

"*Merde!*" Selina exclaimed in annoyance, disentangling herself and draping her red eyed dragon around her as she made her way out onto the landing to the upstairs speaking tube.

"*Merde*!" I repeated under my breath. What it meant I had no idea, but it definitely seemed to express my feelings at that traumatic moment as I searched frantically for Dai's old overalls.

"Oh, it's you," I heard her say, relief sounding in her voice. "Well, Mummy's left the order on the dresser and she says to be sure the chops are here by ten o'clock tomorrow."

"Lloyd the Butcher's delivery boy," she explained briefly as she returned, and the green dragon fell to the floor.

By damn, I learnt more in the next ten minutes than I'd ever dreamt of in the past thirty years, and I don't mind telling you that if it wasn't for those cockles, I don't think I'd have been able to keep up with her! No wonder Darling Gerald looked so bloody anaemic if he had this to contend with, for whatever Selina Rees-Williams had learnt in France, it certainly wasn't just how to speak French! And that chaperoning Aunt of hers from Wrexham had a lot to answer for, you can take my word for it . . .

Chapter 10

"What you looking in there for, Evan?" asked Myra as she noticed me poring over the small type of The Daily Express Modern English Dictionary late that evening.

"Oh . . . just wanted to check how to spell something." She accepted my vague explantion without comment and poured herself another cup of tea from the pot.

It was all right being prepared to act the part of a solicitor and getting all the necessary impressive trappings, but it would be no good unless I could actually sound like one, so there I was searching for a few suitably weighty words to enrich my legal vocabulary. I closed the dictionary with a satisfied snap and rose from the tea table, my head buzzing with my newly acquired vocabulary as I made my way upstairs to change into a clean white shirt and my Sunday black shoes . . . statutory, jurisprudence, edict, advocate, party of the first part, decree, litigation, statute, constitutional, advocate, verbatim, status quo, party of the second part, counsel, whereby, as forthwith . . . the list whirled through my brain.

"Just off then!" I shouted through the passage door. Myra knew that I'd arranged to meet Dai at half past seven, obstensibly for a few drinks. "We might nip over to Harford," I called, "but I won't be late!"

She gave an answering "Cheerio, then!" from the back kitchen.

Even she had been amazed at the amount of cockles I had eaten that tea-time, for Dull Reggie had really done me proud and there'd been a whole bucketful awaiting me when I'd eventually arrived home from building Captain Rees-Williams's stone wall. And after only a few packed sandwiches and a flask of tea for dinner, coupled with the unexpected exertions of the day, I'd been ravenously hungry by six o'clock.

Dai had returned to Tŷ Mawr at about a quarter past one—a bit worried that Sybil hadn't seemed too impressed by the fact that his solicitor was coming to see her that night.

"Wait till I've finished with her boy," I'd re-assured him, "she'll soon change her mind about wanting to marry you—just you wait and see, now." I'd hoped I'd sounded confident.

I had been very tempted to tell Dai all about my unbelievable half-hour spent with Selina and her dragon, but my many experiences of feeling hot under the collar at his irrepressible tendency to push his luck with wide-eyed innuendo and subtle reference whilst in company, regretfully cautioned me against it, even though Selina was returning to 'Aber', as she called it, the following day.

Old Mr. Rees's funeral suit and Pa's travelling desk, spats and spectacles were all laid out ready for me when I arrived at the Coffin Shed just before half past seven. We rarely met at his house since his Mam and Pa had passed on—in fact, Dai spent as little time as possible there himself, preferring the cosiness of his Coffin Shed. Sometimes he didn't go home for days, but well stocked up with food and clothes he was, behind the workbench—even had a folding camp bed tucked away in the corner alongside his cramps. Mind you, he had a lovely house, but I could see he'd be a bit lonely there all by himself. It would be different when he eventually decided to get himself married, but until then, Old Mrs. Ryder came in twice a week to keep everything ship-shape and do his washing and ironing.

It took me but a few minutes to change into my solicitor's garb. Finally, I adjusted Pa's stiff collar, eased the crutch of the rather tightly confining pinstripes to a little more comfortable position, slicked down my hair from a centre parting and stood to attention.

"How do I look then, boy?" I took up a serious pose, disdainfully looking over the top of Pa's spectacles at a grinning Dai.

"Great, man!" he approved, very impressed.

I delivered a few suitably legal utterances liberally sprinkled with some of the ponderous verbage I had recently acquired from The Daily Express Modern Dictionary, and his admiration visibly grew. Mind you, some of it didn't make sense, but it sounded bloody terrific!

"That'll do it, Evan, if anything will," he vowed. "By damn, you really do look the part—and sound it, boy!"

I eased on my stiff, Christmas leather gloves, concealed my somewhat unusual mode of dress beneath Dai's old raincoat, picked up Pa's travelling desk and followed Dai out into the yard.

"The lorry or the bike?" he asked.

I gave a few moments consideration as to which would most suit my newly acquired professional status.

"The bike." I decided.

A pale glimmer from the gas lamp outside lit up the yard as I placed Pa's desk into the sidecar alongside old Mr. Rees's funeral hat. I climbed on to the pillion behind a waiting Dai.

"All set?"

"All set." And off we roared through the gate.

*   *   *

The Public Bar of the Farmers' Arms showed a faint gleam of light as we drove into the yard. Dai took us round the back and we both dismounted. Quickly I discarded the old raincoat, smoothed down my centre parting with a bit of spit, tentatively eased my cramped crutch and placed Mr. Rees's funeral hat in position, while Dai lifted Pa's desk out of the sidecar. Full of nerves he was. Damn, I could see his hands shaking!

"Now, Evan, boy," he fussed, dithering back and fore, "You go on into the old Dairy over by there, see?" I nodded. "And I'll go in and tell Sybil you've arrived. All right?"

"By the way, Dai," I called quietly as he turned to go, "I'm Mr. Forsythe of Hammond, Mason and Forsythe, Solicitors of Cardiff."

"Marvellous," he whispered, "Bloody marvellous."

"And don't forget to say absolutely nothing unless I tell you," I warned as he retreated into the gloom.

I felt a bit nervous myself, mind, as I stood there all dressed up, behind The Farmer's Arms, and a feeling of panic started to rise as I realised that all my impressive sounding, legal jargon had vanished clean out of my head. I made my way across the loose gravel to the door of the Dairy. Cautiously I lifted the latch and let myself in.

A single oil lamp, standing on one of a dozen beer barrels, bleakly lit the cold, white-washed room. I cleared my throat, the noise sounded loud and grating on the chill air and a low murmur of voices filtered in from the adjoining bar as a large tabby cat rubbed itself fawningly against Old Mr. Rees's pinstripes. I tiptoed across the stone flags, placed Pa's desk on top of a convenient barrel near the oil lamp, adjusted the spectacles on the end of my nose and waited.

By damn, those trousers were tight!

A latch clicked, a door opened and in came Dai, tense and

pale, followed by the infamous Sybil of The Farmers' Arms. Full of self-assurance she was, ripe and full-blown and as healthy looking as a randy carthorse. I peered over Pa's spectacles, clasped my hands behind my back and swung up and down on my heels like Jenkins the Schoolmaster—well, it always used to intimidate me when I was a kid, so it was worth trying.

"Wasting your time you are!" she announced as she waltzed around the beer barrels towards me, apparently unimpressed by the severity of my authoritarian pose. By damn, I thought, we're going to have a real battle on our hands with this one.

"I've told him . . ." and she slapped her hand down on top of a barrel, "that . . ."

"Madam!" I interrupted, with what I hoped was a freezing look, "I wish to point out that I, Mr. Forsythe of Hammond, Mason and Forsythe, Solicitors of Cardiff, am utterly unaccustomed to conducting legal proceedings in such a . . ." I paused and brushed an imaginary speck of dust from Mr. Rees's trousers, "such a deplorable place, but force of circumstances, necessary to the safe-guarding of my client's reputation, unfortunately render it unavoidable and I therefore agreed to this meeting." And I wrinkled my nose in distaste, like Darling Gerald when he'd had to ride on Dai's pillion and turned my back on her to open Pa's travelling desk with a flourish.

"Now, you look 'ere," the undaunted Sybil went on, "I've told him . . ."

I whipped round. "Are you referring to my Client, Mr. David Alwyn Rees, Madam?" I enquired coldly.

"Why aye—Dai, over by there. Who the hell did you think I meant then?" And she looked round the room at the silent rows of beer barrels.

"A list of dates, I've got, mind," she smirked confidently and she poked her fingers down into her deep, fleshy cleavage.

She might not have much quality, but, by damn, she certainly made up for it in quantity, I thought admiringly as a warm, crumpled piece of paper was thrust into my hand.

"There!" she said, "What can't speak, can't lie!"

I made a great performance of clearing my throat and proceeded to smooth out the crumpled piece of paper, which read, March 5th., May 7th., June 11th., 12th., 13th., July 21st. and August 14th. All written in rather pale lead.

"I showed them to Dai, didn't I Dai?" she looked over to a wan Dai for confirmation. He opened his mouth to reply when I interrupted with,

"My client has been instructed to remain silent." and Dai closed his mouth again gratefully.

"I'm afraid, Miss . . . er . . . Miss . . .?"

"Miss Thompson," she supplied, with a toss of her thick, wavy hair.

"Well, I'm afraid, Miss Thompson, you must realise," and I gave a disparaging wave of contempt in the direction of the crumpled list of dates, "that this written evidence is completely invalidated unless substantiated by two independent witnesses. Furthermore . . ." I went on before she could get a word in edgeways, "following the precepts laid down in the statutory decree of the law of The Land, I have no alternative but to proceed according to the status quo of jurisprudence regarding accusation of parenthood!" By damn those Daily Express Dictionary words were beginning to flow back fast and furious now, I thought triumphantly, as I meticulously started to array the contents of Pa's writing desk in a business like manner, conscious of Miss Sybil Thompson, reluctant spinster of this parish, watching my every move. She took a deep breath.

"But . . ."

"There is no 'But' Miss . . . er . . . Miss . . .?"

"Miss Thompson," she prompted automatically.

"Thompson," I acknowledged with a deferential bow in her direction, "I must warn you that my client, Mr. David Alwyn Rees has instructed me to instigate proceedings of legal litigation against your person for defamation of character under Sub-section D of the Moral and Social Welfare Act of 1897—which, I might add,—if proved, could incur you in a fine of £50." I heard Dai swallowing hard in the ensuing silence as Sybil blinked a few times, obviously a little stunned by my eloquence.

I pushed my advantage. "You may, of course, seize this last opportunity to relinquish all claims of paternity against my client . . ." Dai and I held our breath.

But Sybil of The Farmer's Arms was a fighter.

144

"No damn fear!" she said defiantly, hands on hips in traditional fearless pose.

Hell, I thought, no wonder Dai couldn't talk her out of it on his own, and there's glad I was that I'd kept my trump card till last. I gave a long, deep sigh and shook my head slowly in condemnation of the rashness of her refusal, then, with great deliberation I retrieved my precious Latin Scroll from Pa's desk and held it out like a sacremental offering before me on the open palms of my hands. I peered over Pa's spectacles, dropped my voice to a reverently low key and intoned . . .

"Then I regret to inform you that once this seal is broke . . . broken," I hastily corrected myself," the Constitutional Legal Process is irrevocably put into motion and it is required by the Law of the Land and His Majesty King George V, that this document be duly registered at the Cardiff Assizes within two days . . . complete with the signatures of the party of The First Part and the Party of The Second Part appended there-to.

Slowly I pulled the bow of 2d. a yard pink baby ribbon open, letting it fall dramatically to the dark flagstones. As Sybil's hypnotised eyes watched in apprehensive fascination I ran my nail under the red sealing wax and broke open the seal—just as the top button of Old Mr. Rees's pinstripes decided to pop off and tinkle loudly on the stone floor at my feet.

I cursed silently under my breath, but Sybil's eyes remained fixed on the yellowing sheet from Pa's old account book which I began to unroll with great deliberation. I placed it carefully on Pa's desk and positioned one of the heavy glass inkwells at the top to prevent its rolling up again. I picked up the pen, dipped it noisily in the ink and motioned Dai forward.

"Mr. David Alwyn Rees, your signature please." Dai stepped forward from the shadows, took the proferred pen with a shaky hand and inscribed his signature on one of my dotted lines. I blotted it meticulously.

"Miss . . . er . . .?" I held out the pen to Sybil.

"Miss Thompson," she volunteered, a bit subdued. She took a hesitant step forward and peered somewhat suspiciously over my shoulder.

"What does it say?" she asked, a hint of apprehension creeping into her voice.

Intoning like the Vicar I began to read . . .

'Variat tamen memoria eius rei. Secundum

nonnullos scriptores ratem longam a terra in
Poeni flumen porrigunt *David Alwyn Rees;*
tum ean ripam . . .'

and as the dramatic story of how Hannibal aided and abetted
by David Alwyn Rees, worked out a way to get his damn
elephants over the river, echoed in the old Dairy behind The
Farmer's Arms, Sybil's confidence visibly began to crumble.

The last Latin prose died away and the pregnant silence
deepened, broken only by the persistent purring of the ginger
tabby as it entwined itself lovingly around my right leg.

"What does it mean?" Sybil whispered.

"It means, Miss Thompson," condescending to remember
her name now that it looked as victory was within sight, "that
unless you also sign this document, relinquishing all paternity
claims against my client, you shall be required to attend a
Court of Law in Cardiff to substantiate your claim—failing
which, as I warned you previously, you will incur a fine of £50
plus £26 legal costs, as stated in the document, to cover my
soliciting." Hell I thought, that doesn't sound right, my Daily
Express Dictionary temporarily letting me down, it seemed.

She swallowed hard. "Well, perhaps I did make a bit of a
mistake," she admitted apologetically, looking round the room
at the silent beer barrel witnesses. "I didn't want to make any
trouble, you knew that Dai, didn't you?"

Dai opened his mouth.

"My client has been instructed to remain silent." I
reproved.

"Yes, well . . ." and Miss Sybil Thompson slowly stretched
out her hand for the pen, took a step forward into the pool of
lamp light and duly inscribed her signature below Dai's.

"Do you know," she added thoughtfully as she handed me
back the pen, "I do believe it must have been Johnny Francis
from Harford then . . . or that Ken Jones from the village . . ."
She walked thoughtfully towards the door, stopped, whipped
round and stared at us both. My heart jumped into my mouth
as I waited . . .

"Where's my damn list of dates gone, then?" she asked, full
of her old bounce once more as she fished in her empty
cleavage and searched the dark flagstones for the elusive piece
of paper. "Oh, never mind," she giggled as Dai and I
obligingly started to join in the search, "I'll just have to make

146

up another lot, won't I?'' And out she flounced with a friendly wave of goodbye.

*   *   *

"Evan boy, you were a bloody marvel!'' Dai breathed with relief as we made our way out into the yard, then just as I was about to put on the old raincoat once more, he gave me a hefty dig in the ribs.

"Did you see who just walked past and went in?'' he hissed, "Old Ken Jones from the village!'' And he slapped his thigh in gleeful anticipation of the unexpected welcome awaiting the poor fellow. "Poor bugger!''he chuckled, "I'll tell you what, Dai, it was a damn good job we went to The Grammar, eh?'' And I echoed his sentiments with heartfelt fervour, after all, it just proves that you never know when a good Classical Education might come in handy.

"Come on then,'' I chivied, "get this bike going, will you, so that I can take these damn trousers off—strangling me they are!''

It was always a bit of a hair-raising experience riding on Dai's Enfield in the pitch dark, as it had the unfortunate distinction that the faster you went the better you could see, as the lights worked straight off the dynamo. Slow down to a safe twenty miles an hour along the high hedged, meandering lanes and you couldn't see a damn thing, so obviously Dai always preferred the alternative and went belting along at forty which was very good for visibility but, because of the numerous 90° bends, was very bad for the nerves!

And as the wide-eyed night owls and the prowling Pembrokeshire foxes pricked up their surprised ears at the sound of our raucous celebratory rendering of Sosban Fach as we speeded perilously along their deserted lanes, I spared a sympathetic thought for poor old Ken Jones who was, without doubt, at that very same moment, desperately trying to find an alibi for every date Miss Sybil Thompson was affectionately confronting him with!

*   *   *

Half an hour later I followed Dai into The Prince in a blissful state of relief at having my own trousers back at last. The bar was surprisingly full for a Monday night, but the reason for the unusual crowd soon became plain when we spied Dull Reggie's Pa in the centre of a throng of back-slapping, drink-treating customers. Always came back to Llanporth to celebrate whenever the news of another offspring reached him through the grapevine. He'd come straight to The Prince off the 7.10 from Carmarthen and with a bit of luck, he might manage to get home by eleven o'clock. Of course, we, also, had to buy him a few congratulatory drinks as well as drinking to our own successful evening, so it was gone ten by the time we eventually pushed our way out through the swing doors.

"The wind's changed," commented Dai, with a bit of a shiver as we strolled back to the yard for me to pick up Pa's travelling desk. "Reckon we're going to have a drop of . . ." He suddenly stopped dead in his tracks, catching hold of my arm, "Look at that, then!" he whispered urgently.

I followed his gaze towards a lightened window. There, silhouetted on the thin curtains was the shadowy, but unmistakable, outline of a closely entwined couple, swaying together in close embrace! Quickly I reckoned up the number of the house.

"That's Umshla's place!" I said unbelievingly.

Dai chuckled. "And that's your Tabitha he's got with him!"

We watched in fascinated amusement as the shadows moved back and forth, twirling and dipping.

"They're bloody dancing!" I whispered hoarsely as the faint sound of music floated out on the chill damp air.

"So that's what he wanted her for . . . but he can't dance, man!" Dai pointed out.

"Well, he's damn well learning now isn't he?" I chuckled, "I hope he doesn't step on poor old Tabitha's feet . . . the left one isn't up to much as it is!"

"She looked realistic, though, didn't she?" Dai remarked as we turned into the yard.

"She did that, boy," I agreed, full of the pride of ownership.

Dai lit the lamp in the Coffin shed and I retrieved my paper bag of solicitor's accoutrements and Pa's travelling desk. "See you at choir tomorrow night then," I reminded.

"I'll be there boy . . . and thanks a million for . . ."

I waved a disparaging hand . . . "See you in court!" I laughed. "Goodnight Mr. David Alwyn Rees!"

"I bid you a very good night Mr. Forsythe," he replied with a formal bow, "And don't forget we're putting a new roof on Mrs. Evans's lav on Thursday afternoon!"

Chapter 11

Miss Gwendoline Davies's extra piano practising had definitely paid off—we'd all ended up together—well, almost together —practically every time and Cy Lloyd, mindful of the word I'd had in his ear before Choir had started, had made a point of congratulating her warmly on the way she'd sorted out her semiquavers so valiantly. And Umshla had echoed, "H . . . h . . . h . . . here . . . h . . . h . . . here!"

I hadn't been able to help noticing as the practice had progressed, how a few of the younger girls were giving Umshla a few surreptitious looks of new appraisal. His terpsichorian activities of the previous two evenings had obviously been observed by some one other than Dai and myself, and the report of the strange event had doubtless spread through the village via the usual channels of the Water Pump Gossipers Brigade. And from the suspiciously speculative way the girls had also eyed each other, it had taken no great mental powers to realise that they were all trying to deduce who his mysterious female companion had been! His reputation and consequently his eligibility were suddenly presenting an entirely different aspect to the unmarried female populace of Llanporth!

"Somebody ought to write and tell his Mam," I'd overheard Mrs. L. Y. T. Jones mutter indignantly to Mrs. Nellie Williams under cover of the long Amen, but I had very much doubted if either would actually put pen to paper.

I grinned at Dai who had also noticed the phenomenon of Umshla's sudden rise to notoriety. "He's booked your Tabitha for next weekend too!" he whispered as Miss Gwendoline Davies flurried her way through the long stacatto introduction to "O Calumny".

"Good for him!" I whispered back as Cy raised his baton to lead us in. Mrs. Ruby Tyler looked over the top of her copy and imperceptibly raised one expressive eyebrow in my direction and I nonchalantly tried to raise one back, but the specialised technique eluded me and to my annoyance I felt both eyebrows shoot up, making me appear, I felt sure, like a startled damn rabbit. I'll practise it in the back bedroom mirror when I get home, I vowed, because, like Latin, you never knew when it might come in useful.

Mrs. Ruby Tyler and her charms had been on my mind

since the beginning of the practice when I'd overheard her mention to Mrs. Evans that her poor Matthew had had to go to Fishguard again that morning for another damn old enquiry and wouldn't be back until the 3.40 the following afternoon and that she'd hoped it wasn't going to become a regular thing. Mrs. Evans had duly sympathised while Ruby had cast a fleeting glance in my direction just to check that I had been listening to her reminder, and to tell you the truth I had temporarily forgotten that she'd told me about Matthew's intended trip at the Whistdrive, Supper and Dance the previous Saturday—well, I'd had such a uniquely busy few days that it was no wonder, after all.

"And I hate making a cup of tea just for myself," Ruby had sighed despondently and Mrs. Evans had agreed and said that it wasn't nice really—didn't taste the same somehow.

The question now was, what was I going to do about it? I mean, compared with the Evan Evans of last week's Choir Practice who had been so cravenly thankful to make his excuses about having to collect important goods from the railway sidings, I was a new man whose veins now ran with the fire of the yellow-footed fruits of the sea. I'll play it by ear, I decided confidently as Cy yelled "Thunder it out, Miss Davies!" as he widely conducted 'Thanks be to God! He laveth the thirsty land.'

The recitatives and choruses went off a real treat that night and our hopes of winning the Martletwy Eisteddfod soared when Cy finally praised us all for our efforts and confidently pronounced that he rated our chances as high, especially if Frank could confine his gastronomic eruptions to the concealing volume of the choruses.

Everyone was in high spirits as we all chatted our way out into the late evening drizzle. The customary shadowy figure stood huddled in the porchway and I suddenly remembered I hadn't paid my debt.

"There you are, Reggie," I whispered, pressing fourpence into his hand. "Well done, boy." I took a quick look round to see if anyone was paying any attention. "More tomorrow?" I asked, pruning my words to an explicit minimum so as not to confuse him. He nodded happily. I cupped my hands together in front of his face as a reminder . . . "Fat ones, mind!"

"Fat!" He beamed back.

A light pressure on my arm made me turn guiltily. The gossiping crowd of choristers thronged about, but the near presence of Mrs. Ruby Tyler was unmistakable and my nostrils twitched instinctively to the erotic aura of California Poppy, although, I must confess, it did fleetingly pass through my mind that it seemed just a shade overpowering, but perhaps it was simply in comparison to that subtle, but never to be forgotten perfume which had enveloped me up at Tŷ Mawr.

By damn, I thought, put cockles and perfume together and what man could resist the inevitable?

"The kettle's still on the hob, Mr. Evans," she smiled, looking not at me but at Jenkins the Schoolmaster's wife who she was busily waving goodbye to. Artful hussy she was, fair play.

"Singing does make you thirsty, indeed," I replied loudly— well—anybody could overhear that innocent remark after all now, couldn't they? And off she sauntered through the quickly dispersing crowd. No time for post mortems, not with the rain coming down heavier every minute.

"Shan't be down at The Prince tonight, Evan," Dai announced hurriedly as he and Ann appeared by my elbow. "The Miss Tugwells have invited Ann and me in for a cup of tea and a piece of cake, so . . ."

"All right, boy," I acknowledged as they waved cheerio. "What did you think of the Bleeding Tree then, Ann?" I called as they started off down the hill.

She stopped and turned with a smile. "The silly old thing had dried up! All that way for nothing?" she laughed.

Lovely girl she was—not a bit like a school teacher, fair play.

*　　　*　　　*

The back lane was pitch black as I cautiously crunched my way over the rain sodden ashes and silently lifted the back gate latch of number 16. Water gushed loudly from a broken chute nearby as I tiptoed up the rain spattered path alongside the immaculately kept back garden. Only ten minutes I'd stayed at the crowded bar of The Prince, just to show my face, but the thought of that simmering kettle on the hob had dulled my usual appreciation of Mick's best ale.

I gave a discreet knock on the back kitchen door and tried to shelter from the steady downpour by pressing myself against the leeward side of the wall.

The door opened.

The low-turned gas mantle hissed a dim, yellow glow, the kettle simmered gently on the hob as promised and pale, smooth arms entwined themselves once more around my neck. No call for Divine assistance this time, I thought exultantly, confidently recalling the dishes of Dull Reggie's cockles I'd eaten for breakfast and tea.

"Who's been giving you lessons, Evan Evans?" Mrs. Ruby Tyler managed to gasp a few minutes later.

I ignored the question.

The mantelpiece clock ticked the minutes quietly away, the kettle came to the boil and I eventually came to the conclusion that coconut matting couldn't hold a candle to a spring interior. Not that I was complaining, mind you, it was just a bit harsh on the knees that's all.

"By damn!" she sighed admiringly as we eventually sat at her chenille covered table sipping our steaming cups of tea, "You've improved since last week, Evan Evans!"

And mindful of my enriched experiences in the realms of continental technique and my increased stamina resulting from my new diet, I had to agree I had! Hellfire and Blinding Lights, *I had*!

Chapter 12

It was a week before Christmas and my predictions of a hard winter had proved correct, with sales of long woollen underwear and fleecy lined liberty bodices rocketing to rival the lucratively selling garments of Alice and Maud. The Llanporth Choir had achieved their well deserved success in winning the Martletwy Eisteddfod, when Miss Gwendoline Davies had played the piano as she'd never played it before. Thanks to Tabitha the St. John's Ambulance Team had won the local area cup with the outstandingly high standard of their bandaging, narrowly beating Glynmawr to second place. Umshla had continued his secret weekly dancing sessions until the beginning of December when his Mam had returned home from Pontypridd, Miss Sybil Thompson had succeeded in getting Johnny Francis from Harford to the altar early in October—Ken Jones obviously having proved a bit too wily for her, and old Mrs. Rees the Farm took her last journey in the Tudor-carved coffin one cold grey morning in early December. Ann and Dai had eventually managed to catch the Nevern Tree actually bleeding, following two weeks pelting rainfall in mid-November, little Bertha Gwillam, in desperation at the increasing weight of her noble perambulator and rapidly growing baby, had finally admitted defeat and transferred her bonny infant to a carrying shawl and Lloyd the Stationmaster had, on an outing to Swansea, purchased a miracle cure for flatulence, but it hadn't done any good. Mrs. Dago Jones and Dull Reggie had continued their taxi-pram service outside The Prince for Old Dago throughout the bleak winter Tuesday and Saturday nights while The Child that was Born on the Sabbath Day continued to thrive and prosper along with the nits and lice and kittens in the little cottage up on the hill.

And me? Well, after that traumatic week in September I'd considered it prudent to cut down my cockle intake a trifle, as events were beginning to get just a little out of hand, and I had reluctantly rationed myself to one helping a day as a precautionary measure to diminish the side effects, pleasant though they had been! Because, fair play you can't carry on like that now, can you? Not in Llanporth anyway. In retrospect I am only just beginning to realise how unbelievably lucky I was that The Pump Brigade never got wind of the symptomatic behaviour of my cockle fever. Over done Mrs. Dago Jones's prescription I must have—too keen, you see.

Captain and Mrs. Rees-Williams continued to honour us with their presence at the Whistdrive, Supper and Dances, while Selina, according to their reports, was astounding everybody in Aberystwyth University—something which I could well believe!

We were walking huddled arm in arm for warmth against the freezing night air, making our way towards the Church Hall for the Grand Christmas Dance. And walking on air we were, Myra and me. Only an hour before Myra had returned from the evening surgery with the long-awaited and unbelievably wonderful news that I was going to become a father at last, and we had both been in a euphoric state of sheer delight ever since and were looking forward to telling all our friends the good news. That whip and top were going to be put into good use earlier than I had ever hoped, I thought gleefully as I pushed open the Hall door and dutifully handed our tickets over to Jenkins the Schoolmaster who was keeping a wary eye out for any gatecrashers from neighbouring villages—it had only happened once before, mind, and that was over ten years ago, but he'd been on guard against a re-occurence ever since and now we always had special tickets printed for the Grand Christmas Dance.

The Church Hall was tinselled and decorated almost beyond recognition—even the Union Jack had red paper roses pinned all over it. Diamante necklaces sparkled and best imitation pearls gleamed on every bosom, silver and satin dancing shoes peeped out from under chiffon, *crêpe-de-Chine*, satin and silk frocks (most of which had started life on Alice and Maud I was pleased to note). Masculine chins gleamed stubble-free smooth from razors freshly strapped behind kitchen doors and stiff white collars chaffed mercilessly into newly scrubbed pink necks. The Llanporth townsfolk were all dressed up to the nines for the greatest social event of the year and Dull Reggie, now sporting long trousers as befitted his new station in life as a school leaver of a week's standing, hugged himself with delight as he gazed at the colourful, noisy throng from his usual corner by the door.

"Let's tell Dai and Ann," Myra whispered excitedly as soon as we'd hung up our coats and changed our shoes. Dying to tell everybody she was, and I couldn't blame her—tickled pink I was myself!

We made our way towards them.

"Congratulations, boy!" Dai exclaimed on hearing our news, slapping me resoundingly on the back ". . . and you Myra, of course!" he added hastily.

We all laughed—we'd have laughed if somebody had recited the A B C so elated we were!

"And we're going to call it Megan if it's a girl and Evan if it's a boy," Myra announced proudly.

"Go on then, Ann," Dai suggested, giving Ann a nudge. Ann smiled, a really happy smile it was.

"Show them, then!" he urged impatiently.

Ann held out her left hand and Myra gasped with suitable admiration and pretended surprise, at the twinkling diamond ring on her third finger.

"Bought it in Swansea, this afternoon," Dai proclaimed, flushed with pleasure.

More joyful congratulations and kisses followed as Mrs. L. Y. T. Jones bustled past to greet Umshla who had just come rather nervously in through the door.

"I'm terribly sorry, Mr. Watkins," she apologised awkwardly, "But there's no whistdrive tonight—just dancing, you see. I'm terribly sorry!"

"I . . . I . . . I . . . know," he stammered, turning deep beetroot. Mrs. L. Y. T. Jones looked taken a-back.

Suddenly she spotted the shiny new pair of patent dancing shoes poking out from a torn paper bag under his arm and obviously remembered the stories she'd heard about his nocturnal activities.

"Oh . . . oh . . ." she said lamely, "Oh . . . that's all right then—as long as you know . . ." and off she drifted to meddle somewhere else while Dai and I chuckled to ourselves.

"I hear congratulations are in order, all round!" And there was Mrs. Know-All Jones, her eyes swiftly darting from Myra's waistline to Ann's finger. Amazing, it is, how news gets about, I thought just as Jenkins the Schoolmaster blew a blast on his whistle and announced the First Waltz. Dozens of couples poised themselves at the ready for the first step as Miss Gwendoline Davies, resplendent in pink sateen, lowered the needle into position on the gramophone. Then, to everyone's amazement, across the floor strode a determined Umshla, his nerve obviously screwed to the limit, his new patents squeaking at evey step.

Over to the gramophone he went, bowed stiffly and asked an astonished Miss Davies to accompany him in the waltz. So flustered she was that I thought for a moment she was going to faint. Then pulling herself together she tucked her new lace-edged hankie (bought from the shop that very afternoon for 1½d.) into the expanding bracelet of her watch, rose shakily to her feet and was immediately enveloped in Umshla's well practised grasp as he swept her off into a rigid one, two, three round the room, his mouth moving slightly as he conscientiously counted the beats.

"Well!" gasped Myra, "Talk about a dark horse!"

"I bet she feels a bit softer than Tabitha!" chuckled Dai in my ear. "Come on Ann—let's join 'em." and off they danced.

"I'm just going to pop outside for a minute," Myra whispered, "You know . . ."

"But you only just went before we left home!" I pointed out in surprise.

"I know . . . but . . . oh, well, it must be the excitement!" she laughed and she disappeared through the back door to pay a visit to the largest tombstone in Llanporth Churchyard.

"Good evening, Mr. Evans."

I turned at the greeting.

"Good evening, Mrs. Tyler—Mr. Tyler!" I replied with a formal smile, my nostrils twitching at the conflicting aromas of California Poppy and T.C.P.

"Just going round to tell a few friends our news," Mrs. Ruby Tyler simpered. She paused slightly and Matthew Tyler smiled smugly.

"We're expecting a Happy Event in the early summer, you see!"

I coughed, half choking as a sudden intake of breath went down the wrong way.

"Con . . . congratulations!" I managed to stammer as I shook them both by the hand.

"Yes," Mrs. Ruby Tyler went on, "And if it's a girl we're going to call her Rose and if it's a boy we're going to call him *Evan!*"

I felt the blood drain from my face.

"After Matthew's dear Father," explained Ruby sweetly, and off they both sauntered to impart their joyful news to the next group of chattering bystanders, leaving me slowly recovering from the shock—not that it's got anything to do with me, I tried to assure myself resolutely.

"That feels better!" giggled Myra at my elbow. "Now, let's have a dance before the gramophone runs down!"

It was just after the tango that Captain and Mrs. Rees-Williams accompanied by an elegant Selina and her Darling Gerald, came sweeping into the hall with a cold breath of night air. Jenkins the Schoolmaster hurried over to greet them and the Vicar and his wife almost bowed and curtseyed their welcome.

It was just after the following Valeta that Old Jenkins blew three dramatic blasts on his whistle and proceeded to inform the assembled crowd that Captain Rees-Williams asked for their attention as he had a special announcement to make.

There was a hub-bub of speculation and interest as we all wondered what it could be. Captain Rees-Williams stood to attention beneath the rose festooned Union Jack and cleared his throat. The whispering died away expectantly.

"It is with great pleasure that I, and my good lady wife, wish to announce the engagement of our only daughter, Selina, to Mr. Gerald Llewellyn—of the Wrexham Llewellyns," he pointed out with a satisfied smile "And we would like to wish them every happiness for the future upon this happy occasion."

And everyone murmured surprised congratulations and beamed at the happy pair.

Captain Rees Williams held up his hand for silence.

"And . . ." and he gave a condescending smile round at everyone, "You all know how impatient this young generation is . . ." and everyone murmured sympathetic agreement that they knew exactly how impatient the young generation was "so, it is therefore, with extreme," and he repeated it, "extreme pleasure that Mrs. Rees-Williams and myself," and he bowed to Mrs. Rees-Williams who gave a sickly smile back, "wish to announce their forthcoming wedding on January 17th in the Parish Church, where our good vicar has agreed to officiate at the ceremony."

There was a stunned silence. You could almost hear

158

everybody think 'that's bloody quick!' as they mentally counted up the months for future reference. Me included!

Jenkins the Schoolmaster started a lonely clap and we all joined in thankfully, all smiling brightly and saying how lovely it was. Old Jenkins frantically tried to signal to Miss Gwendoline Davies to go and wind up the gramophone, but she was gazing rapturously into Umshla's eyes and hanging on to his every stammered word, so in exasperation he had to dash over and do it himself, almost forgetting in his haste to blow his whistle to announce that the next dance would be a Ladies' Excuse Me. And everyone gasped Oh with delight as we only had a Ladies' Excuse Me at the Grand Christmas Dance as Jenkins the Schoolmaster considered it a bit too frivolous for the regular Whistdrive, Supper and Dances.

Myra and I were just one-stepping round by the door, with Myra chattering about the astonishing news, when there was a tap on her shoulder and there stood Miss Selina Rees-Williams, smilingly excusing her. Myra stepped away graciously and cast her eyes round for a suitable partner to excuse herself.

"Er . . . congratulations!" I murmured, self-consciously, stepping awkwardly on her toe as I missed a step.

"Thank you Mr. Evans," she smiled.

"Er . . . I suppose you won't be going back to Aberystwyth University now then?"

"No, dreary old place, it is," she declared, dismissing 'Aber' with a shrug, "I know what they're all thinking!" she giggled suddenly, her voice sounding a little less *crachach* than I remembered it.

"Oh . . . no . . . no!" I disparaged in a most gentlemanly manner, my voice sounding suitably aghast.

"They're right, mind! End of June it's due!"

"Oh!" I said inadequately.

"And if it's a girl I'm going to call her Myfanwy and if it's a boy . . ." Oh, no, I thought, not again!

". . . I'm going to call him . . . *Evan!*"

She watched the effect of her pronouncement on my face, enjoying the look of consternation which I knew was written all over it.

". . . after Daddy's brother," she added mischievously, "He's a Captain like Daddy! Au revoir!" she waved as Ann tapped her on the shoulder and took her place for the last few bars. By damn, I thought, what a bloody night! A shattered wreck I'd be by the end!

It was with relief I heard Old Jenkins blow his whistle and ask the gentlemen to accompany the ladies into the Supper Room. Glad of a sit down, I was.

We sat round the Christmas decorated, food laden table, the customary Welsh cakes being replaced by traditional mince pies.

"Friends!" Mrs. Rees-Williams, having regained some of her slipped composure, rose to her feet at the top of the table. "Before we start our Christmas fare," she went on, fingering her pearls fondly, "the Vicar has a little surprise for us all—he has kindly arranged to provide us with an extra treat to gladden our Festive Supper!"

I looked round at the ham and boiled potatoes, the pickles and the trifles, but could see nothing unusual, when, over from the gas rings stepped the smiling Vicar and his good wife, both bearing, with the reverence of a golden chalice, two enormous, steaming dishes . . . of fat, juicy, yellow-footed cockles!

Everyone cheered and Myra breathed, "Oh, Evan! Your favourite!"

I smiled weakly.

Round to each person in turn they went, serving the cockles to an accompaniment of Oohs and Aahs and what a surprise, etc.

"Cockles, Mr. Evans?" intoned the Vicar reverently, spoon at the ready.

I stared bewitched into the steaming bowl and my past life flashed before my eyes.

"Er . . . no thank you, Vicar!" I heard myself saying, "I think," and I took a regretful sigh, "my cockling days are over . . . I think I'd better stick to the ham!"

And I cut myself a lovely, succulent slice of Cy Lloyd's best ham, gave Myra an affectionate wink and sank my teeth into the juicy meat with relish.